Call Me Oklahoma!

MIRIAM GLASSMAN

Holiday House / New York

To the wonderful teachers I've been lucky
to have, beginning with my parents

Library of Congress Cataloging-in-Publication Data

Glassman, Miriam.
Call me Oklahoma! / by Miriam Glassman. — 1st ed.
p. cm.
Summary: Paige Turner starts fourth grade with a new name in
hopes of being more bold and brave, especially when dealing with
class bully Viveca and overcoming her stagefright.
ISBN 978-0-8234-2742-0 (hardcover)
[1. Self-confidence—Fiction.   2. Names, Personal—Fiction.   3. Schools—Fiction.
4. Family life—Fiction.   5. Bullies—Fiction.]   I. Title.
PZ7.G4814355Cal 2013
[Fic]—dc23
2012023971

Contents

Acknowledgments

Many thanks to the wonderful faculty and community of writers at Vermont College of Fine Arts, especially Margaret Bechard, who helped me shape this story; to Julie Amper at Holiday House who made working on this book pure pleasure; and to Ann Tobias for all her guidance in getting it there. Special, humongous thanks to Julia Glassman for her keen eye, good humor, and extraordinary patience with her technophobic mom. My deep gratitude also to my husband, Steven, and daughter, Emily, for their sustaining support, wit, and love.

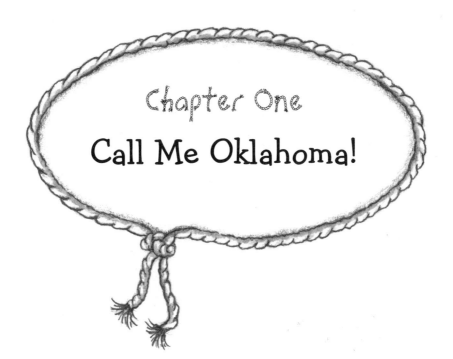

Chapter One
Call Me Oklahoma!

On the first day of school, Paige Turner came down to breakfast and announced that she had changed her name. "From now on," she said, "call me Oklahoma!"

Her mother looked up from her crossword puzzle, astonished, and the pencil in her hand dropped to the floor.

Her father looked up from pouring his coffee, and it dribbled all over his travel mug.

But her brother, Conrad, digging in a box of Corn Zappies for the free prize inside, said, "Oklahoma? What kind of a *dumb* name is that?"

"It's not dumb," Paige replied, twisting the red bandanna around her neck. "It's a *good* name."

"Are you for real?" Conrad said, his hand crunching around the cereal. "You actually *want* to be named for the forty-sixth state, with more man-made lakes than any other?" Paige's older brother had a head stuffed with little-known facts. He said it came from reading all the magazines in the waiting room at his orthodontist's.

"Conrad does have a point there," said Paige's mother, picking up her pencil and erasing a long line of boxes. "Besides, people don't just pluck a new name out of the air on their way to breakfast."

"I disagree," said Mr. Turner, tightening the lid on his travel mug. "If Paige wants to be Oklahoma, why not? In fourth grade, I was Mortimer."

"Mortimer?" gasped Mrs. Turner. Paige and Conrad looked equally horrified.

"Well . . . only for about a month. And there's a chance this might last just as long," their father said, winking at their mother. He picked up his briefcase and travel mug and kissed Paige on the top of her head. "This certainly is a dinger!" he told her. "But you have yourself a great first day...Oklahoma."

"What's a dinger?" asked Paige.

"A surprise," said Mr. Turner, and put his hand out to give Conrad's hair a farewell scruffle. But just before making contact with Conrad's head, he noticed the hair gel and jerked his hand back. "New look, eh?" said Mr. Turner, patting Conrad's shoulder instead.

Paige wished her father didn't have to leave so soon. She needed someone around who understood her goal. Because of course the moment the garage door shut, Conrad started in on her.

"So why'd ya pick a dumb name like Oklahoma?"

"Because," said Paige, and that was all. But as she tipped the heavy carton of orange juice over the edge of her glass, the voice inside kept going. *Because I'm starting fourth grade. And I'm different now.* Unfortunately, even the voice inside squeaked on the word *different*. Still, Paige was determined that this year *would* be different. *She* would be different. More like her cousin Cordelia!

Cousin Cordelia lived across the country in Berkeley, California, and during the summer, the Turner family had visited Aunt Joni and Cordelia. Paige thought her cousin was amazing. For one thing, Cordelia cartwheeled everywhere—even in the living room. *Even* after her mother yelled at her to cut it out. Cordelia also climbed up open doorways like a human spider and ate artichokes, which she called ogre tongues. And when the mean boys on the street teased her, Cordelia pinched her nose and said, *"Eww,* what's that stink? Oh, the neighbors must've put out their garbage!"

Paige wished she could be more like that. And on the long plane ride home, she decided she not only *could,* but *would.* The first thing she'd need, however, to become a more Cordelia-ish kind of person was a different name. A name with guts.

Oklahoma was a name with guts. It reminded Paige of the cowboys shouting *"Yee-haw!"* in the musical they'd seen during their visit. The show was called *Oklahoma!* and it was full of cowboys and spunky women twirling around. The music had Paige bouncing in her seat, and at the end of the show, when all the people onstage waved their hats and yelled *"Yee-haw!"* Paige felt so full of joy, tears sprang to her eyes. She longed to be the kind of person who yelled *"Yee-haw!"*

"I like the name Oklahoma," said Paige quietly. "It has...guts."

"Yeah, right," laughed Conrad. "Like you could pull off a name with guts. You still run into closets during thunderstorms!"

"Do not!" snapped Paige, and began blowing angry juice bubbles in her glass, pretending each popping bubble was Conrad disappearing into thin air. *Pop!*

Unfortunately, he was still there, pulverizing their new box of cereal into Zappie dust, all for some stupid, junky prize.

"That's enough, you two," said Mrs. Turner. She got up from the table and set down two bowls and a carton of milk. "Let's get this show on the road. You don't want to be late for the first day."

Paige grabbed the cereal box from Conrad and scowled at him. *She* knew she'd be different this year. She already felt different in her bright-blue T-shirt and brand-new cargo shorts. The shorts had a million Velcro pockets that made a satisfying *zwip!* whenever she ripped them open. And her grandma had sent her a pair of bright-red clogs that drummed out a joyful, clompy sound as she walked. Like tap shoes, only better. Paige couldn't wait to clomp loudly down the shiny tile floors at school. Everyone would know when Oklahoma was coming!

Paige adjusted the bandanna around her neck and dug into her cereal. Not only did she have a new look, she had a new outlook. With every loud crunch of cereal, she felt more determined to be a different person. So different, even Viveca Frye wouldn't tease her.

Viveca Frye thought she was the boss of everyone because she could kick the ball farther than anyone in the grade. She also had a way of saying "what*ever*" that had most of the girls following her around as if she was the Mayor of Cool. But acting like the boss of everyone wasn't the worst thing about Viveca. The worst thing was how she'd made Paige feel after last year's spring assembly.

The entire third grade had been onstage for the annual Third-Grade Poetry Slam. Paige's poem was about squirmy snakes that "squiggled like a silent *S* in the woods." But the moment she opened her mouth, all her words squirmed away! She couldn't remember a single line. She could barely remember what her poem was about. So she did the only thing that made sense. Just like the snakes in her poem, Paige squiggled "like a silent *S*" as fast as she could off the stage. She was such a nervous wreck that as soon as she got backstage, she threw up—right onto her teacher's shoes.

She could still hear the chorus of "*Eww,* gross!" from the other kids as they jumped away. It was absolutely the worst moment of Paige's whole, entire life.

For the rest of third grade, Viveca never let her forget it. "Wow, look at how fast Paige runs!" she'd shout at recess when they played kickball. "Almost as fast as she did when she ran offstage and went *blaaaaagh* all over the teacher's shoes!"

But this year would be different. This year, Paige would be the kind of person who wouldn't get teased, who wouldn't be afraid of being onstage, or thunderstorms, or *anything.*

"Well, I'm not calling you Oklahoma," Conrad said, his hand diving back into the cereal. "It's stupid."

"But that's not fair! You got new sneakers! Why shouldn't I have a new name?"

"You can't compare sneakers with a name!"

"Besides," said their mother, silently counting letters with her pencil point and then writing them into her puzzle, "Paige is a beautiful name. And," she added, looking up, "it's a family name. There's always been a Paige in the Turner family."

"Eureka! I've found it!" Conrad shouted. "It's a glow-in-the-dark compass yo-yo!" His face lit up as he pulled a small package from the cereal box and tore it open. "Lookit!" he said, and holding the compass yo-yo in the palm of his hand, turned himself east, west, north, and south. "Hey, it really works!" Then he stood on his chair and pressed the yo-yo against the light over the table. "Let's see if it glows!"

"Conrad Turner, you'll burn yourself!" snapped Mrs. Turner, swatting her son's hand away from the light-bulb. "And don't let your father hear you getting so excited over a cereal box yo-yo." Mr. Turner was the director of small toys development at the Whoopee-Yahoo Toy Company.

"But, Ma," whined Conrad, "this one has a real compass. None of Dad's has that."

"Conrad Turner," his mother said with a fiery spark in her eye, "that is a cheap, gimmicky yo-yo with an inferior string. If your father sees you spinning that thing around here, well, you know he's bound to get all wound up. Now, c'mon, you two. Eat up! We're not on a summer schedule anymore." She smiled down at her puzzle. "Hey, here's one for you, Paige: a six-letter word meaning 'metamorphosis.'"

Paige tapped the tip of her spoon against her teeth and thought for a moment. She remembered last year when her class had done a big unit on metamorphosis. They'd learned about things in nature that changed—like caterpillars into butterflies. "Change?" she said.

"Bingo!" said Mrs. Turner, writing in the word. "Good work, Bug."

"*Oklahoma.*"

Mrs. Turner ignored her and, looking up from her puzzle, studied Conrad's hair. "Conrad, did a brush actually make contact with your head this morning? Or did you just wave it in the vicinity?"

"*Maaa,*" he whined, "it's gelled! You don't brush gelled hair!" Paige giggled as she poured some more cereal. So she wasn't the only one who wanted to make some changes.

"Paige, do you have your emergency house key?" her mother asked.

"In my backpack!" Paige replied. "But I'm not Paige anymore. I'm *Oklahoma.* Okay?"

Conrad rolled his eyes. "What're you going to do when the teacher takes attendance? If you don't answer

8

Ms. Hardy, she'll send you to the principal's. Whoa, the principal's office on the first day!" He flashed his hideous green-and-yellow braces at Paige, and for a moment, her heart froze with fear.

She turned to her mother. "You could write a little note for me, right? Please, oh, pretty please?"

Mrs. Turner regarded Paige with raised brows and tight lips.

"Just a weensy note?" begged Paige. "Like the kind you write when I have a doctor's appointment. I even know the perfect paper to use!" She scurried over to the kitchen drawer where the Turners shoved all the stuff that didn't have any other place to live. "Here," said Paige, presenting her mother with a small pad of paper. "This one always makes teachers smile."

Mrs. Turner looked at the pad with the tiny, colorful shoes dancing around the border and shook her head. "Sweetie, I'm not writing any notes about silly name changes." Then she got up from the table and packed her tote bag with her daily container of cottage cheese and fruit, and shoved in her unfinished crossword. "Well, everyone," said Mrs. Turner when she was all packed up, *"Carpe diem!"*

Paige looked puzzled. "What's *carpay deeum*?"

"It's a quote from Horace, a poet who lived a long time ago, in ancient Rome. In Latin, *carpe diem* means 'seize the day!'" Mrs. Turner was an editor and had been working for months on a book of famous quotes.

9

"But what does 'seize the day' mean?" asked Paige.

"It means take advantage of all that this day has to offer!"

Conrad slurped and crunched the last of his cereal, then jumped up with his prize. "Seize the yo-yo!" he shouted. "Let's see if it glows!" And he ran to the front hall closet and slammed the door. Paige trailed Mrs. Turner to the hall, hoping she could change her mother's mind before she left.

"Hey, it works!" yelled a muffled closet voice.

Mrs. Turner glanced at the closet door and rolled her eyes. Then she leaned down to kiss Paige good-bye. Paige was still sore about the note. So she kissed her mother back, but it was the kind of kiss without much feeling behind it.

As Paige clomped into the dining room for her backpack, she thought of asking Conrad to write the note. But then she remembered his handwriting. It was atrocious, even for a sixth grader. Each word looked as if it had survived a terrible accident, and no teacher would ever believe a grown-up had written it. Thinking about Conrad, she shook her head. *Useless,* she thought; *utterly useless.* It was up to her to tell her teacher she had a new name.

To cheer herself up, Paige unzipped her backpack and breathed in the exhilarating aroma of fresh school supplies: one new box of markers, two dangerously pointy pencils, two sherbet-colored notebooks—one in raspberry, one in lime—and one metallic purple folder. And in the outside pouch of her backpack, the blue rubber lightbulb her father had given her. "The marketing department just isn't sure what to do with a rubber lightbulb," he'd told her. "It doesn't seem to have any purpose other than being blue and rubbery. But I kind of like it for that." Paige liked it, too. In fact, she loved the blue rubber lightbulb and had known the moment she saw it that it would bring her good luck. It had already brought her some humongous, ginormous, fantastic luck: Viveca Frye was not on her class list! *Yes!* Fourth grade would be the best year ever. Now all she had to do was show everyone that over the summer, Paige Turner had changed into a brave new Oklahoma.

Chapter Two
Oklahoma Seizes the Day

"C'mon, Tennessee. You're too slow," whined Conrad. He was already half a block ahead of Paige.

"Wait up!" Paige shouted. "And don't call me that!" It was hard to keep up with Conrad. There were a bajillion bug bites up and down Paige's legs, which meant she had to stop every few steps to scratch them. The worst one was on the knuckle of her big toe, and the only way she could scratch it was by stomping down hard onto her own foot. She looked down at her scabby legs. *Ugh!* What she needed was cowboy boots. Not only would they cover all the scabs and bites, but boots would truly make her feel like Oklahoma. "Conrad, wait up!" she yelled. "And my name's not Tennessee! It's Oklahoma!"

Some of the other kids on their way to school heard this and laughed. But Paige ignored them and ran to catch up with her brother. His eyes were fixed on his compass yo-yo, and he'd started walking in the wrong direction. Paige yanked his sleeve. "This way!" she said.

Conrad shrugged her off. "I was just testing something." But Paige knew her mother was right. The compass yo-yo was a piece of junk.

As soon as the crossing guard waved them across the street to the Guggenheim school, Conrad shot off toward the sixth-grade doors, where his friends were waiting. Paige stood by herself in the school yard, stomping and scratching all her itches. She watched the smiling mothers snapping photos of their kindergartners. Some of the kids looked smaller than the backpacks sticking up behind their heads. Kindergarten was a big deal for them. But for Paige, fourth grade would be even bigger.

She scanned the school yard again and her heart zoomed at the sight of her best friend, Gavi. She ran toward her.

"Paige!" Gavi shouted, as soon as she saw Paige. The three little braids hanging down over one side of Gavi's face were capped with colorful beads that clacked softly whenever she turned her head. "I'm so pumped we're both in Ms. Hardy's class!" Gavi said. She bent her fingers back in a way that made them clack softly, too, since she was double-jointed.

"I know!" said Paige "It's the best!"

Lily and Mackenzie came running over. Lily was still as short as last year, but Mack had shot up over the summer and now towered over all of them. "Hey, I like your new glasses," Mackenzie said to Gavi.

Gavi fiddled with a corner of her red frames. "Yeah, well, it was time for a new look."

Lily pointed down at Paige's feet and squealed, "Ohmygosh, I love your clogs!" Lily bounced around like a jumping bean. "I've got erasers that look just like them!"

"That's not the only thing new about me," said Paige, trying to sound light and breezy. Her heart was pounding and her tongue felt as dry as a whiteboard eraser. But this was it. If things were going to change, she had to seize the moment. "I've decided to change my name," she said quickly. "From now on, call me Oklahoma!"

Gavi squinted through her glasses. "Did you say Oklahoma? As in the *state*?"

Paige nodded. "I know. It's a real dinger!"

Mack looked at Lily and Gavi. Lily looked at Gavi and Mack. Then Lily fixed her gaze on the bandanna around Paige's neck. "Are you, like, trying to be a cowgirl or something?"

Paige shrugged. "I dunno," she said lightly. "Maybe."

Gavi pursed her lips and nodded slowly. "I get it," she said, as if she'd just cracked a secret code. "You've picked a new identity. Cool! I read a *lot* about spies over the summer, and secret agents do that all the time. So you're sure you want to be Oklahoma?"

Paige nodded. Lily looked at Mack as if she was waiting for directions.

"Okay," said Mack. "Hey, get it? O K. That's the abbreviation for Oklahoma!"

"Oh, can I call you that?" Lily asked, hopping up and down.

Paige bit her lip. "Hmm...I don't know." She hadn't thought about nicknames. And she wasn't sure about being called O K. "Maybe just stick with Oklahoma."

"Okay," said Gavi, shrugging up her backpack. "I mean, not, like, O K—just *okay*....okay? Oh, man! I'm super-confused. And it's only the first day!" The bell rang, and Gavi, Paige, Lily, and Mack headed inside for another school year.

"Bummer that we're not in the same class," said

Mack, and the girls all nodded sadly as they walked down the hall.

When they arrived at Mack and Lily's classroom, Lily turned to Paige and Gavi. "Well, this is it," she said, and pressing the back of her hand against her forehead sighed. "Parting is such sweet sorrow!"

"Till lunchtime, then?" said Gavi as she and Paige walked backward down the hall.

"Till peanut butter with Fluff!" cried Mack.

"Till that weird grainy bread with seeds my mom keeps buying even though we all hate it!" said Paige.

"Till then, till then! Sweet sorrow and farewell!..."the four friends shouted, waving.

Outside room 3, their new teacher stood at the door to greet them. "Welcome, fourth graders!" she boomed. Ms. Hardy was a large woman with seriously big hair, and standing before her, Paige felt like a tiny elf. Could she tell a giant she had

16

a new name? Unsure, Paige stomped her itchy foot and slipped quietly into her new classroom.

Room 3 was full of bulletin boards covered with red-and-orange paper leaves and signs with questions like WHO AM I? and WHAT IN THE WORLD? Mobiles swayed lazily in the warm classroom air, and the room buzzed as everyone showed off their new school supplies. One kid had a pen with six different colors. Another had a pencil case that played "The Chicken Dance." Cynthia Sobkin had a cool gel pocket on her notebook that turned different colors depending on her mood.

Paige found her desk. Her name was written on a piece of paper with tape over it. *Well,* she thought, *this is the first thing to take care of.*

At the desk next to her sat Sanjay Patel. Sanjay had been in Paige's class every year. Last year he'd not only joined the trend of wearing stickers on his face, but had worn one every day of school.

"Hey, Sanjay!" Paige said, and leaned toward him to get a better look at the lightning bolt zigzagging down his nose.

"Hey there, Paige." He was lining up a long row of colored pencils on his desk.

Paige took out a pen to cross out her name. But before she did, she leaned over to see who would be sitting on the other side of her.

"That's *my* desk," a voice boomed overhead. Paige looked up.

Viveca Frye!

"But I thought...you were in the other class."

"My mom had me switched," said Viveca. "She says Ms. Hardy is the best fourth-grade teacher. So you know..." Paige stared up at Viveca. The girl must've grown five feet over the summer! Paige clenched both of her shorts pockets, and without thinking yanked them open with a loud *zwip!*

"What was that?" said Viveca, looking around.

Paige shrugged. "I don't know," she said, and quietly pressed her pockets closed. Her stomach quivered, but she reminded herself that she was Oklahoma now. And Oklahoma wasn't afraid of Viveca. Unfortunately, her stomach still belonged to Paige.

As Viveca settled into her seat, she stared at Sanjay.

"What are you looking at?" said Sanjay.

Viveca rolled her eyes. "I can't believe you're still wearing stickers. That's so *over.*" Sanjay touched a finger to his lightning bolt and stroked it gently as if to comfort it. Viveca then spread out a brand-new set of fifty glitter markers.

"Wow!" Paige exclaimed. She decided not to take out her box of twelve plain, boring markers.

"Each one has a different smell," said Viveca. "*This* one's banana-nut pudding." She pointed to the pale-yellow cap. "And *this* one's grape-pop-fizz...and this one's chocolate-sprinkle cupcake...."

Paige's mouth began to water like crazy. "Can I taste...I mean, smell one?"

Viveca's hands slapped over the markers. "I'm only sharing them with my friends," she said as she leapt from her seat with a fistful of markers, and headed across the room to Cynthia Sobkin. Cynthia cooed over Viveca and her markers, and soon a swarm of girls was buzzing around Viveca.

Paige looked at the name taped to her desk and rolled her own boring, nonsmelling pen back and forth. *Come on, pen,* she thought. *You can do it. Just cross out* Paige *and write in* Oklahoma*!* But her pen wouldn't budge.

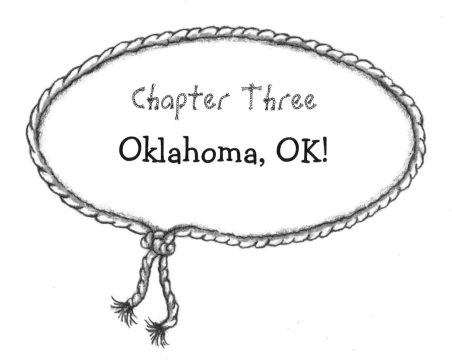

Chapter Three
Oklahoma, OK!

"Okay, here we go!" Ms. Hardy sang out as she kicked up the doorstop.

Viveca rushed back to her seat, and Paige twisted around so she wouldn't have to look at her. She dug out her blue rubber lightbulb and gave it a squeeze for good luck.

Ms. Hardy strode to the whiteboard and faced the class with her hands on her hips. "First of all, I'd like to say welcome to the fourth grade!" She had a nice, twangy way of speaking, kind of like the characters in *Oklahoma!* "As most of you know, my name is Ms. Hardy. But over the summer I married a most wonderful man, Mr. Wilson. So now I have a new name."

Paige's hand unclenched her rubber lightbulb. Her

teacher had a new name, too? Paige sat up straight, and her eyes didn't leave the board as Ms. Hardy's hand skated the marker across it, writing:

Ms. Hardy-Wilson

Then she swept a line beneath the words. It looked like a little stage, and Paige imagined her teacher's new name taking a bow. "Now, for all you inquiring minds," the teacher continued, "I'll tell you two things about my husband, Mr. Wilson. One: he can recite the alphabet backward faster than anyone you'll ever meet. And two: he makes a really mean BLT. That's a bacon, lettuce, and tomato sandwich—for those of you who didn't cover that in third grade." She let out a deep, hearty laugh. *"Hah-hah-hah-hah-hah!"* It was a little scary, because Ms. Hardy-Wilson was not only very tall with seriously big hair, but also had enormous teeth. She reminded Paige of a large bear.

Ms. Hardy-Wilson then told them about some of the exciting things they would be doing in fourth grade: multiplying fractions, using calculators, learning about the solar system and natural disasters, writing with "Vivid Vocabulary," and taking a virtual tour of the United States. "Oh, and we can't forget one of my favorite events, the Fall Variety Show!"

Viveca turned and rolled her eyes at Paige. Paige tried to swallow, but her throat felt as if it was stuffed with a rubber lightbulb.

"So," said their teacher, "now that you know a little about me and fourth grade, I'd like to get to know all of you!" She scraped a chair to the front of the room, sat down, and flipped open her attendance book.

Paige's heart took off. It was just like being on the diving board at the town pool. Trembling, she would clench her toes over the edge of the board and then stare down into the deep end while everyone behind her yelled *"Jump! Jump! Jump!"* But she always wound up walking back, head down, off the board.

This time, though, there was no turning back. She had to take the plunge.

Ms. Hardy-Wilson called out students' names and before long she was at the *P*s. "Sanjay Patel?" she said.

"Here!" called Sanjay, and everyone laughed when he wiggled his stickered nose. A bunch of *P, R,* and *S* names rolled by, like distant thunder in Paige's ears.

"Paige?...Paige Turner?" Ms. Hardy-Wilson's eyes scanned the room.

"She's right here!" yelled Viveca, pointing. Paige stared like a trapped mouse—a trembling trapped mouse. "Well, hey there, Paige!" Ms. Hardy-Wilson said, flashing her large, toothy bear smile.

A kid from the other side of the room shouted out, "Hey, Paige Turner, turn the page!"

Paige slumped in her seat. *Oh, no! Not another year of page jokes!* She took a deep breath and sat up. "Um, Ms. Hardy-Wilson?" Her voice quavered, but she pushed on.

"Um...could you please call me...O...O...oh, never mind!"

Room 3 fell silent. All eyes were now fixed on Paige.

In a gentle voice, Ms. Hardy-Wilson asked, "Is there a different name you'd like to go by?"

Paige's heart beat so fast she was sure it was going to bust straight through her rib cage and ruin her new shirt. But if she chickened out now, she'd be Paige for another whole year. Her toes curled tightly inside her clogs. "Um," she squeaked, "could you please call me... Oklahoma?"

Her teacher's brows rose like a kindergartner's drawing of two mountains. *"Oklahoma?"* she said. "As in the forty-sixth state, with more man-made lakes than any other?" Paige was dumbstruck. She wondered if her teacher and Conrad had the same orthodontist.

"Yeah, and can you call me New Jersey?" a boy shouted across the room.

"Call me Nebraska!" yelled another kid.

"Hey, I wanna be Wyoming!" A wave of laughter rolled across the classroom, with Viveca's laugh crashing down loudest of all. Paige looked over at Gavi. She wasn't laughing. She was flashing Paige the OK sign with her thumb and forefinger.

Paige nodded back at her, but her face burned and a rubber-lightbulb-sized lump sat in her throat. *Don't cry,* she told herself. *Just don't cry.*

Ms. Hardy-Wilson rose to her full grizzly-bear

height. "Room three, hush!" The class snapped into silence. "There is nothing wrong with preferring a particular name. I have asked all of you to call me Ms. Hardy-Wilson instead of Ms. Hardy. And if Paige prefers that we call her Oklahoma, well then, that's what we'll call her." Paige's body temperature rocketed to about ninety billion degrees. She hoped she wouldn't melt all over her seat.

"Each one of you," continued Ms. Hardy-Wilson, "has many possible selves inside you. And discovering those possible selves is an adventure that will last you a lifetime. Take joy in your discovery! You never know what you'll find."

She looked straight at Paige and said, "I admire your individuality and creative flair, Miss Turner. Oklahoma is a fine name. And a beautiful state. It's also a place where you can get an outstanding BLT." Ms. Hardy-Wilson looked down at her attendance book, crossed out one name, and wrote in another. "There," she said. "All set, Oklahoma." And she gave Paige a little wink.

Paige sat back, shaky as a bowl of Jell-O. But it was the good kind of shaky. She had declared herself Oklahoma in front of her entire class. And in front of her grizzly bear of a teacher, too.

She put her lucky lightbulb inside her desk and unloaded the rest of her school supplies. Then, turning her back to Viveca, she crossed out the name PAIGE on her desk and wrote in plain, boring red marker, OKLAHOMA.

She had to squish in the last few letters, but she didn't care.

"Do you really think you can be Oklahoma just like that?" said Viveca.

Paige shrugged. She wasn't sure. But this desk belonged to Oklahoma. And that was a start.

Chapter Four
Oklahoma vs the Boiled Brain Nuggets

Though Paige Turner had seized the first day at school, seizing the ones that came after was much harder. For one thing, her family kept forgetting to call her by her new name. Conrad was the worst.

"Hey, Pennsylvania," he said at supper one night. "Pass the butter?" Paige put her hand on the butter dish and kept it there. "Oh, sorry," said Conrad in a fake-polite voice. "I forgot. Pennsylvania, would you *please* pass the butter?"

Paige's hand didn't move from the butter dish. She glared at Conrad. "Say it."

"It," replied her brother.

"Not *it*. Say my name."

"My name," said Conrad.

Paige gritted her teeth. *"Oklahoma."*

"Oh, are we playing the states game?" said Conrad. "Then I guess the next one would be, um...Oregon!" And so it went.

Mrs. Turner sighed and pressed her fingertips on either side of her head. "Could we please not have this battle of wills at every meal?"

"Taking on a new name isn't easy," said Mr. Turner. "But I admire your stick-to-itiveness." Paige smiled at her father. She was glad someone in her family understood.

"Yeah, but even with a new name, she's still a mouse," said Conrad. He fixed his eyes on Paige's plate. "I bet you're even too scared to eat that cauliflower."

Paige aimed her meanest face at Conrad, then looked down at the cauliflower. How in the world did her mother expect her to eat something that looked like boiled brain nuggets?

"Go on," her brother pressed. "If you're so brave and gutsy, *Oklahoma,* eat it. Go ahead...chow down!"

Paige scowled fiercely at Conrad. Inside, however, she was experiencing extreme cauliflower terror. As the official Picky Eater of the Turner

Try Our Boiled Brain Nuggets

family, Paige had a body that was a well-trained army. Every taste bud on her tongue had joined forces with her throat to build a fortress no cauliflower could push through. She'd experienced this kind of combat a zillion times before. But now Paige had to fight herself. If Cousin Cordelia could gobble up ogre tongues, Oklahoma could gulp down a few brain nuggets.

She speared one of the boiled atrocities with her fork. She brought it so close to her face her eyes crossed. When she uncrossed them, she saw that her entire family was watching her. *You can do this,* she thought. *You can eat strange foods, no matter how gross. Oklahoma's gonna break through the old, picky Paige barricade and ride that cauliflower train straight down!*

"Well?" said Conrad.

Paige sniffed the spongy mass at the end of her fork. The nasty boiled brain nugget smell shot straight up her nose, and she shuddered. Maybe it was better not to look. She closed her eyes, took a deep breath through her mouth, and brought the brain nugget up close enough to tickle her lips.

Her eyes flashed open and... *Oh, no!* She felt herself weakening. She couldn't hold on! The brain nugget's grossitude was overpowering. Her throat clamped shut. Her fork clanked down.

Oklahoma could eat anything, *anything* but boiled brain nuggets.

"*Seeeeee?*" said Conrad.

Paige gave a low growl. "So what if I don't eat cauliflower?" she said. "You don't eat asparagus."

Conrad shrugged and speared some of the cauliflower with his fork. "Course not," he said. "Asparagus are gross."

"But that's not fai—"

"Well," said Mrs. Turner, getting up from the table, "too bad we don't have time for that debate. Your father and I have to get moving. It's Meet the Teacher Night." Mr. Turner pinched the bridge of his nose and shook his head wearily. He'd been coming home late from work all week and wasn't in the mood to be rushed through his supper.

"You mean Meet the *Creature* Night," said Conrad, food spewing from the corners of his mouth.

"Well, maybe your teacher is a creature," said Paige. "But mine is really nice." She turned to her parents. "So if you're both going out, who's sitting? I hope it's Liza." Liza was in high school and let them eat ice cream straight out of the carton.

"Well, I thought this time we'd leave Conrad in charge," said Mrs. Turner. "It's just for a couple of hours. I think you two can handle that."

"*Me?*" said Conrad, his eyes as round as dinner plates. "You want *me* to babysit?"

Paige sat very still. This was an outrage.

"Well, we thought we'd try it out this once," said Mr. Turner. "As a kind of trial run for the future."

Conrad beamed, flashing his yellow-green braces at

Paige. *Yilchh! What a monster mouth.* How could this be happening? When had Conrad moved up from being baby*sat* to baby*sitter*? No one was going to suddenly make Paige the baby. Oklahoma was *not* a baby.

"I'm not a baby!" Paige blurted out.

Mrs. Turner rinsed her plate and slid it into the dishwasher. "Of course you're not," she said. "We know that."

"Yes, of course, we know that," her father echoed, glancing at his watch and shoveling food into his mouth.

"We just want Conrad to take more responsibility at home," said Mrs. Turner. "If any little thing ever happens when we're out, we want Conrad to know how to manage it."

Paige's heart pumped fiercely. Conrad's mouth hung open; nasty little bits of food clung to his braces. It made Paige think of dead flies in a spider's web.

"Mmmff," agreed Mr. Turner. His fork scraped across his plate in wide, noisy arcs, shoveling in as much as possible before Mrs. Turner could take the plate away.

"But that doesn't mean he's the boss of me...right?" said Paige.

Her parents exchanged a look. "Well—" Mr. Turner said, lifting his fork.

Mrs. Turner finished his sentence for him as she whisked his plate away. "Conrad is in charge of making sure nothing dangerous happens."

Paige's breath was fuming so heavily through her nose, there could've been flames shooting out of it. She stormed away from the table to the piano in the living room. Adjusting herself on the bench, she pounded out her scales. When she was done with that, she quickly organized her fingers into a protest song. And as her fingers hammered the keys, the words to her song marched inside her head:

Conrad's not the boss of me,
I'm not some little baby!
Conrad's not the boss of me,
I'm not some little baby!
They shouldn't leave him here with me.
He never lets me watch TV,
And always says my shows are dumb—

Paige's fingers stopped and then restlessly tapped the keys as she searched for a rhyme: *Crumb, glum, strum, gum* . . . She liked *crumb* best but couldn't figure out how to use it. So for the moment, she went with *glum.*
The whole thing makes me really glum.
The lyric wasn't quite what she was looking for, but it would have to do for now. And at least it let her surge ahead to her rallying finish:

Con-rat, Con-rat,
Ick, ick, ick!
Con-rat, Con-rat,
Ick, ick, ick!

After making her anger musically clear, Paige took out her slowest, saddest piece of music. Her piano teacher,

Mrs. Klonsky, was from Russia and mostly taught Paige cheerless Russian songs. The melodies were so droopy and grim, Paige's parents often shouted from the kitchen, "Can't you play something *happier*?"

At the end of the heavy-hearted étude, Paige's weary fingers collapsed onto the keys. First cauliflower, and now Conrad babysitting. She went upstairs, crashed onto her parents' bed, and, grabbing all the pillows, made herself into a Paige sandwich. "Maybe I should go with you to Meet the Teacher Night," she said to her mother from in between the pillows. "I could show you where my classroom is and wait outside. I'll be very quiet. I can walk all the way down the hall on tippy-toes, even in my clogs."

"I don't think that's a good idea," said her mother, removing the earrings she'd worn to work and fishing out a different Meet the Teacher pair in her jewelry box. Outside, it was dark, and rain tapped lightly against the windows.

"Y'know," said Paige, "if you leave Conrad in charge, he'll just stay in his room the whole time playing computer games. The really noisy ones. He won't be able to hear anything, not even a robber breaking into the house."

Mrs. Turner sighed. "Conrad has homework to do," she said. "I'll see to it that he isn't plugged into some game while we're gone. And you'll be fine. You can always call if you need us." Her mother squirted cologne onto either side of her neck, and then onto Paige.

As her mother walked downstairs, Paige trailed her, desperate to find a reason not to leave Conrad in charge.

"You'll be *fine*, Paige," her mother said, reaching for a light jacket.

"Has anyone seen the good umbrella?" her father asked from inside the front hall closet. *That's it!* thought Paige. *Rainstorms!* But before she could launch into a lecture on the dangers of driving at night in the rain, the front door slammed and her parents were gone.

Chapter Five

The Cottage Cheese Monster

"So," said Conrad after he and Paige had argued about who would load the dishwasher and who would clear the table. "You wanna make up phone numbers like 1-800-Booger and see what we get?"

"Nooo!" replied Paige.

"But I'm *in charge*," said Conrad. "We have to do what *I* want."

"Mom and Dad didn't say you're in charge of everything."

"Yeah, just you, Arizona." Conrad opened the refrigerator and slung his arm over the door as if he was waiting for his favorite TV show to come on.

"Don't do that!" Paige shouted. "You should never touch a refrigerator during a storm! Lightning can come right through!" She thrust her hands out toward Conrad like a deadly bolt. "And *zap!* You're fried!"

Conrad ignored Paige's pantomime and pulled out a tub of cottage cheese. "Eureka!" he said. "I've found it!"

Paige made a face. "Cottage cheese? Yuck! How can you eat that stuff? It's so...lumpy."

"Are you kidding me? It's *gooood,*" said Conrad, pulling the top off the container. "In fact, this is what Little Miss Muffet ate on her tuffet. Curds and whey. That's what they used to call cottage cheese back in the Old Mother Goosey days!"

Paige sighed. Conrad and his factoids. But for a moment, she wondered which would be worse—eating curds and whey or having some large, hairy spider plop down beside her.

"And another thing not a lot of people know about cottage cheese," continued Conrad. "It's *magical.*"

Paige gave her brother a withering look. "It's cottage cheese," she said. "There's nothing magical about that."

"Oh, yeah? Well, every time Mungo eats it, he turns into a monster."

"Mungo? Who's Mungo?"

"You never heard about Mungo?" said Conrad, taking a spoon from the drawer. "Mungo is this kid—a lot like me. Really excellent, and always does the right thing.

Like, he almost never cleans his ears with the butter knife or blows his nose in the towels." Paige giggled in spite of herself.

"But, see, even though Mungo is nearly perfect and his parents' favorite"—Conrad stabbed the white lumpiness with his spoon—"the moment he has one spoonful of cottage cheese…" Conrad slid the spoon into his mouth. His eyes closed, and a smile spread across his face before he yanked out the spoon and said, "…something *strange* begins to happen."

Conrad's body twitched as if he was suddenly overcome with painful spasms. The spoon fell from his hand and clanked on the tile floor. Gasping and groaning, Conrad climbed up and stood on the kitchen counter. "And then," he said, "before he even knows what's happened, Mungo becomes…a dis*gus*ting, *hid*eous, *drool*ing *monster!*" He spread his arms wide, bent his fingers into claws, and bared his horrible yellow-green teeth.

"*GRAHH!*" he roared, leaping off the counter at Paige.

Paige screamed and shot off toward the stairs. Roaring and growling, the Cottage Cheese Monster clomped after her, his arms stretched stiffly in front of him. Screeching with laughter, Paige bolted up the steps. The monster nearly caught her by her ankles, but she managed to leap a few inches ahead of its claws.

Thunder exploded over the Turner house and Paige screamed again. *Oh, no!* The only thing worse than a thunderstorm was being alone with Conrad in a thunderstorm. Just as she neared the top of the stairs, a huge *ka-BOOM!* shook the house, followed by an earsplitting *ka-CRACK!* And then *ZAP!* Everything

went black.

Paige shrieked. Her hands slapped the tops of the steps as the monster's footsteps stomped behind her.

"Wait!" growled the monster. But Paige was too terrified to stop. She reached the top of the stairs, lurched toward the bathroom, hit the wall—*"Yowch!"*— and then threw herself into the bathroom and slammed the door.

In the darkness, the only thing Paige could focus on was the *ka-BOOM ka-BOOM* of her heart. It was beating so fast, she feared she'd use up a whole lifetime of heartbeats in a single night. She willed her frantic heart to calm down and took lots of deep, slow breaths. Her piano teacher called them "cleansing breaths." In through the nose—*sniff!* Out through the mouth—*ahhh!*

But even through her cleansing breaths, thunder kept pounding and rumbling in Paige's stomach. A chill tingled through the hair on her arms. But she couldn't be like a mouse and hide, shivering in the bathroom. That would just prove Conrad was right. She took another deep breath. "What would Oklahoma do?" She'd take control. *What we need here,* Paige thought, *is a flashlight.*

As she headed out of the bathroom, the house was quiet. She wondered where the Cottage Cheese Monster had gone. It was hard to tell. All she could hear was the rain pounding the windows as the next batch of thunder growled around her.

Feeling her way along the walls, Paige found her room. She tripped over her backpack lying on the floor but caught herself before she could fall. *Now just find your way to your desk,* she told herself, and pretending she was in a cave, she took the final, careful steps to the lost treasure. She was concentrating so hard on not bumping into furniture, she forgot to worry about the storm.

When her hand finally gripped the hard, smooth corner of her desk, she grasped the drawer knob and found her flashlight. The batteries still worked! Aiming the flashlight down at the floor, she followed the comforting circle of light out of her room. As she went in search of Conrad, she imagined the rest of the house as the cave of the Cottage Cheese Monster.

"Mungo?" she called out. No answer.

"*Mungo?*" she called a little more loudly. "*Conrad?*"
Still no answer.

No doubt the monster was crouched in some dark corner, waiting for the right moment to pounce on Paige with its slimy, cottage-cheesy claws.

But she was Oklahoma now. And no way would Oklahoma walk into the trap of the Cottage Cheese Monster.

Feeling deliciously sneaky, Paige tiptoed into Conrad's room—the last place he'd expect to find her. She swept the beam of light around and checked that the room was empty. The thunder had faded to a distant rumble, and while Paige sat on Conrad's bed waiting for him to get bored and give up, she pointed her flashlight straight up and put her hand over the circle of light. It was fun projecting her fingers onto the ceiling. When she pulled her hand back a bit, the shadow on the ceiling became a giant hand. She wiggled her giant hand around and imagined it picking up Viveca and dangling her from high above. "Put me down!" Viveca would plead. And Paige, the giantess, would mutter, "What*ever,*" and toss her down. A smile spread across Paige's face.

Suddenly, the lights flashed on as every appliance in the house started beeping and buzzing back to life. "Oh!" squeaked Paige. She jumped off the bed, and her foot landed on something alive!

"*Owww!*" The pained squeal from the floor sent Paige leaping wildly into the air with a loud shriek. When she looked down, she saw it was Conrad's hand she'd stepped on. And now the rest of him was inching out from beneath his bed.

"*Con*rad?"

"Geez! Watch where you step!" he growled, and stood up.

"What were you doing under there?" Paige asked him. The moment the words were out of her mouth, she knew.

Paige took a hard look at him. He was so pale his freckles stood out like marker dots on a white piece of paper.

"I—I was just looking for something," he muttered, searching around his feet for the "something."

"You were scared," said Paige.

"Was not," Conrad said, jutting out his chin. "I was looking for the compass yo-yo."

"And?"

"It's not here."

Paige gave her brother her toughest Oklahoma squint. She looked him up and down, from his dust-covered pants to his pale, frightened face. "Call me Oklahoma," she said, "and I won't tell anyone you're scared of the dark."

"*WHAT?*"

"Say it."

"Oh, man!" Now Conrad's face was flushing pink.

"Say it, and I won't tell any of your friends you were hiding under your bed."

Conrad brushed past her, bumping her arm as he

went to the door. "Geez...man!" And then mumbled miserably, "Oklahoma."

"What's that?" said Paige. "I couldn't hear you."

"*OKLAHOMA!*" Conrad shouted. *"THERE! Y'HAPPY?"* And he slammed the door behind him.

Paige smiled at the closed door. Yes she *was* happy. And with a quiet *"Yee-haw!"* she clicked off the flashlight and went downstairs. She definitely deserved a reward, like maybe a Fudgsicle. Or better yet, a marshmallow kabob. Almost anything, Paige decided, except cauliflower—or cottage cheese.

Chapter Six
Jinxed!

"Pretend you're a windmill," said Gavi. "And this huge wind comes along and blows you in a circle...like this!" Gavi launched into a perfect cartwheel, rotating across the lawn three times, and then popped up firmly on her heels. Paige tried to imagine herself as a windmill, too, but the moment her palms crushed into the cool grass, it was as if the wind had crumpled her to the ground.

It was Thursday. Paige always went home with Gavi on Thursday, until one of her parents picked her up. Today, she and Gavi had had a picnic snack of super-chocolaty brownies, and then they'd practiced cartwheels in the backyard, because as Gavi said, "A person named Oklahoma should know how to do a decent cartwheel. Especially after yelling '*Yee-haw!*' Secret agents need them, too."

"*Cartwheels?*" asked Paige. "Why do secret agents need to know how to do cartwheels?"

"For confusing the enemy, of course," said Gavi. And she threw herself down into a cartwheel so fast and so close to Paige's face, Paige leapt back with a gasp.

"Wow! Guess you're right about that."

Even though being Oklahoma wasn't about confusing the enemy, Paige agreed that a few confusing tactics might come in handy. Unfortunately, they were hard to use on Viveca Frye. Viveca had her own confusing tactics, and she seemed bent on turning Project Oklahoma into *Mission: Impossible*. For one thing, she didn't just refuse to call Paige Oklahoma. She'd started calling her Biloxi.

"Why are you calling her that? It's not even a state," Gavi said as they got ready for math. "It's a city."

"Who cares?" said Viveca. "My uncle lives in Biloxi, and that's way more fun to say." A few of the other girls in the class twittered and copied Viveca in calling Paige Biloxi.

It drove Paige nuts. While Ms. Hardy-Wilson wrote the math problems on the board, Paige scribbled cursive *Z*s all over her notebook. Cursive *Z*, she'd decided, was a very satisfying letter to write when you were really, really mad. With all its sharp, ferocious zigzags and the big, huffy loop at the end, it made her hand feel as if she was swishing a sword—*swip, swip, swip!*—in a duel with Viveca.

After math, Gavi came over to Paige's desk and, looking down at the forest of *Z*s on Paige's notebook, asked, "What's all that?"

"That's how I feel about Viveca," Paige whispered. "That girl makes me broiling, sizzling, cursive *Z* mad!"

"Then why don't you just go back to being Paige? Maybe if you stuck with your old identity, she wouldn't pick on you so much."

Paige scowled up at Gavi. "But she picked on my old identity!"

"Hmm." Gavi nodded. "True. But becoming Oklahoma hasn't changed that. Well, not yet, anyway. Just seems like you've given her something new to tease you about."

Paige shook her head adamantly. "No. Once Viveca sees that I'm becoming more of an Oklahoma, things'll be different. You'll see." Gavi shrugged.

Why couldn't Gavi understand how important it was for her to stick to being Oklahoma? Sure, it was hard and sometimes made her cursive *Z* mad. But it was worth it, and she would stick to her goal, no matter what. Sticking to her goal, however, became especially hard later that morning when the class lined up for music. Paige was chatting with Gavi and Sanjay about a funny TV show they'd all watched the night before. Sanjay was trying to remember the name of one of the characters.

"Oh, wait, I remember now!" said Paige. "It was Buddy!" But just as she said it, Viveca whipped around and said the name at the exact same time.

"Personal jinx!" Viveca shouted, pointing straight at Paige. Gavi and Sanjay looked stunned. A personal jinx was like being under an evil spell. You weren't allowed to speak until your name was said by the person who'd jinxed you. Viveca glared at Paige with jinxy glee.

"No way, Viveca!" Paige blurted out. "You can't do that!" It felt great to shout "No way!" at Viveca, even while her heart pounded like a sneaker in the dryer.

For a moment, Viveca looked truly surprised. But only for a moment. And then her face melted back into calm as she counted on her fingers: "One, two, three, four, five, six, seven. You just said seven words. So now I have to say your name seven times for you to get unjinxed." She sucked her teeth with satisfaction as their teacher gave the signal to file quietly down the hall.

In the music room, Paige's class always sat on a large blue rug. Paige wiggled all the way to the back. This way, she could hide behind Elwin Diggins, with his huge head of unbrushed hair.

The music teacher, Mrs. Tipton, stood behind her piano, waiting for the class to settle down. Mrs. Tipton was tiny and looked about a thousand years old. She was like an old auntie who pinches cheeks and acts as if all kids are two-year-olds. But she was so sweet and smiley Paige couldn't dislike her.

"Today we're going to learn a new song!" Mrs. Tipton told the class. "This is a song you can sing anywhere in the world and people will understand you! I'll play it for you first, and then you follow along. Here we go."

Ging-gang, gulli, gulli, gulli, gulli, watcha,
Ging-gang, goo,
Ging-gang, goo,
Ging-gang, gulli, gulli, gulli, gulli, watcha,
Ging-gang, goo,
Ging-gang, goo.

"Now you try it!"

The kids of room 3 looked at each other. What kind of nutty song was this? Paige couldn't think of any country where they would understand it. She didn't understand it herself. It was gobbledygook.

As Mrs. Tipton played the music, the class tried to mumble along. It didn't even sound like singing. It sounded like a room full of people muttering to themselves in a strange, ancient language.

Mrs. Tipton clapped her hands.

"*Nonononono!* I can't hear the words! I tell you what. Back row, please stand. Each of you will sing one line."

Sing? Paige wasn't even allowed to speak. Her eyes searched the room for help. But all she found was Viveca's eyes shooting powerful personal-jinx rays straight at her.

"Miss Turner, we'll start with you," said Mrs. Tipton. But Paige could barely hear the piano's plinking over the wild drumming in her ears.

Then, suddenly, an idea pushed its way through. Placing a hand on her throat, Paige swallowed hard and made a pained face.

Mrs. Tipton stopped playing and peeked over the top of the piano. "Miss Turner, I can't hear you. Sing out, dear!" Paige poked at her throat. Opening her mouth very wide, she mouthed the words *Can't sing! Laryngitis!*

"Ohhh. I see," said Mrs. Tipton. "Well then, let's start with the next person." A huge breath of relief whooshed out as Paige looked over at Gavi, flashing her a thumbs-up.

After all the rows had slogged through their *gullies* and their *watchas*, Mrs. Tipton said, "We have a little time left over. Does anyone have a song they'd like to suggest?" Gavi's hand shot up. "Yes, Miss Williams?"

"I think we should sing 'Oklahoma!'"

Paige's heart gave a joyful leap, and she flashed Gavi a double thumbs-up. Three minutes of singing "Oklahoma!" and Paige would be jinx-free!

Mrs. Tipton shuffled through her music sheets. "Well," she said, "'Oklahoma!' is a fine, rousing song. But I don't have the music for it here. Any other suggestions?"

Viveca's hand shot up. "Since it's so close to Halloween, how 'bout we sing 'Funny Li'l Pumpkin Face'?

Everyone groaned. "Funny Li'l Pumpkin Face" was a second-grade song. But it had a lot of yelling and stomping parts, so Viveca liked it.

"Splendid idea, Miss Frye!"

Paige gave Gavi a thumbs-down and slumped behind the hedge of Elwin's hair. She should have known that becoming a braver and more daring person wouldn't be as easy as just changing her name to Oklahoma. One quick zap from Viveca, and she was back to being a mouse. A mouse who wasn't even allowed to squeak!

For the rest of the morning, Viveca made sure everyone knew that Paige was personal-jinxed. Everyone stared at Paige with pity, keeping far away from her as though the jinx was contagious.

At lunchtime Paige took a few bites of her sandwich, but the jinx made it hard it swallow. Fortunately, Gavi had her pen with her. "Spies always need to be prepared to take notes," she said. So Sanjay, Gavi, Lily, Mack, and Paige traded notes back and forth, trying to figure out ways to unjinx Paige. But when a big blop of jelly from Paige's sandwich fell onto the paper, their conversation ended. Paige crumpled up the paper and left the table to throw it away.

Being forbidden to speak, she was in no rush to get back to the table. She lingered by the trash barrel and across the cafeteria watched Viveca yakking away, her hands diving down to grab someone's pack of Gummi bears. Paige suspected she was trying to trade desserts. And she'd get her way. As usual. Sure enough, the boy sitting across from Viveca handed over his Gummi bears, a sight that made Paige broiling, sizzling, cursive *Z* mad.

As she dragged her feet back to her table, she thought about her teacher telling her that Oklahoma was a fine name, and that she should discover all the possible selves inside. Paige knew that included a self that didn't give up.

When she was back at the table, Paige signaled to Gavi for a pen and scribbled a message on her napkin. The message was so long, she had to use both sides. Then she handed it to Gavi.

"I don't know if it'll work," Gavi said after reading the napkin with Sanjay, Lily, and Mack.

"It's a great idea!" said Lily. And Mack agreed.

"I'll do my best!" said Gavi.

"Me too," said Sanjay.

After lunch, Ms. Hardy-Wilson asked the class to take out their social studies books and read silently about the states of the Midwest before their discussion. Gavi raised her hand. "Ms. Hardy-Wilson? Can I sit with Paige?" Paige held her breath.

"*May* you sit with Paige? Sure," said their teacher. Paige let out her breath as Gavi moved her chair.

As Viveca opened her social studies book she smiled smugly at the silenced Paige. Paige quickly looked down at her own book.

"Viveca," said Gavi, "do you know what page we're supposed to start on?"

"Twenty-nine," replied Viveca.

"Are you sure? I think you'd better check with the teacher." Gavi gave Sanjay a quick, sharp jab with her elbow. Viveca shrugged and raised her hand. "Ms. Hardy-Wilson, what page are we supposed to start on?"

"Everyone should begin on page twenty-nine."

"Viveca!" whispered Gavi. "Ask her what page we're supposed to read *to.*"

Viveca snorted and raised her hand again. "Ms. Hardy-Wilson, what page should we read to?"

"I've put the page numbers on the board, Viveca. Are you having trouble seeing them?" Paige looked up from pressing cursive *Z*s into her notebook. Sure enough, there were the page numbers on the board. *Dang.*

Gavi squinted. "Viveca, I can't read the board from here. I think these new glasses aren't right. The zeros look like sixes, and the threes look like eights. Can you tell me the pages?"

"Pages twenty-nine to thirty-two and thirty-six to thirty-eight, and then forty-three to forty-five," snapped Viveca.

"Whoa! Say that again," said Sanjay. "And *slo-o-o-wly.*
I need to write that down." Paige bit her lip and tried not
to laugh.

Viveca rolled her eyes. "What*ever,*" she said. "Page
twenty-nine to page thirty-two. Then page thirty-six to
page thirty-eight. And page forty-three to forty-five! Got
that?" And she banged her book up like a fortress in front
of her face.

"Thanks, Viveca!" said Sanjay.

"Yeah, and thanks for unjinxing Oklahoma!" said
Gavi, smiling over at Paige.

Viveca's nose rose over the top of her book. "What
are you talking about? I didn't say her name." She shot
Paige a nasty look.

"You said *page* eight times," said Gavi. She flashed
her notepad at Viveca to show how she'd kept track.

Paige put a hand to her throat and smiled. "That
means I'm unjinxed—with one left over!"

"Yeah, but I said *p-a-g-e,* not *P-a-i-g-e.*"

"Same thing," said Sanjay. "I think it's called a
homonym."

"I know that, stickerface. Doesn't matter. 'Cause she's
not Paige anymore. She's *Oklahoma.*"

"That's not what it says on her official school record,"
said Gavi, taking off her glasses and cleaning them with
the edge of her shirt.

Sanjay nodded. "You can ask the principal if you don't
believe her."

"And," said Paige, "most of my family still calls me Paige...even though I keep telling them not to." Never before had Paige so enjoyed the sound of her own voice.

Viveca looked around at them. "What*ever!*" she snapped, and went back to her reading.

"*Ahem,*" coughed Ms. Hardy-Wilson, towering over Viveca. "Is this posse having trouble with the assignment?" For a moment everyone stared silently down at their books.

Then Paige looked up. "Um...we had a little trouble finding the right page," she said. "But now everything is O.K"

Chapter Seven

Oklahoma Flips

Paige managed to stay jinx-free, though Viveca still refused to call her Oklahoma. Paige tried not to care too much. She wore a bandanna around her neck every day and clomped noisily down the hallways in her red clogs. She liked hearing the other kids say "You always know when Oklahoma's coming!"

At recess she got together with Lily, Mack, and Gavi. They had a special game called Keesters. Whenever they sat next to each other one of them would say "Move yer keester!" and bump the other one's hip. It made them laugh, even if there were only two of them. And when it was the four of them, it was hilarious. One time, after being bumped, Mack farted, taking the game to a whole new level, beyond hilarious. They kept hoping that moment would happen again. Even without the extra sound effects, Paige loved the game just because she liked saying *keester*. It sounded like a very Oklahoma-ish word.

At recess, Gavi suggested they play a round of Keesters and then spy on people.

"Oh, sorry. Can't today," said Paige, heading over to the jungle gym. "I need to practice my flips. Another time, okay?" Paige had always been afraid of flipping on the bars, even the low ones. And of course, Viveca loved teasing her about it. But not this year. Paige would stick to her goal and learn to flip over the jungle gym bars—even the high ones. She imagined Cousin Cordelia flipping over the top bars, and told herself: *That's what Oklahoma would do, too.*

As Gavi, Mack, and Lily looked for a bench to play Keesters, Paige stood in front of the jungle gym and took a deep breath. *You can do this,* she told herself. *These are just the baby bars.* Grasping the lowest bar, she scrunched herself up, closed her eyes, and . . . *flip!* Over she went.

Paige opened her eyes. *Hey, easy-peasy!* She climbed a little higher but could still touch the ground on tippy-toes. She gripped the bars, hoisted herself up into a crouch, and imagined someone giving her a push. *Flip!* Over she went!

She decided the next level up was still borderline baby bars. So she climbed up two more levels and looked down. Unless she was a giant, her feet couldn't touch the ground. And if she jumped or let go, she'd definitely break her legs. Good. She was officially High Up.

Paige turned to face the highest bar and grabbed it. But the moment her fingers wrapped around the warm metal, it was as if someone had stomped on the gas pedal of her heart. Really hard. All she felt was sheer terror.

Be a monkey! she told herself, and hoisted up her knees so that she was scrunched into a tight ball. *Good!* She shut her eyes and, imagining someone pushing her, began to roll forward. She was halfway through the flip, with her belly pressed flat against the bar, when suddenly, everything stopped.

The imaginary pusher had run away. Even worse, the imaginary pusher had left Paige hanging over the bar, staring down at the rubber mat a million miles below.

Push! Flip! But her body refused. It was as if Paige had instantly turned from monkey to sloth. She was stuck, doomed to hang over this bar for the rest of her life!

Some kids gathered below, and the bars vibrated as they began climbing and flipping. When someone jumped on the low bars, the vibrations caused one of Paige's clogs to fall off. It clanged against the bars and clonked down onto Elwin Diggins's head.

"Hey!" Elwin shouted up at her. "You can't throw your shoes at people! I'm telling!"

"I didn't throw it!" Paige whispered down at Elwin. She didn't want to shout for fear that the vibrations of her voice would cause her to slip and fall. So in a tiny

voice she added, "It fell off my foot."

Elwin picked up the clog and looked up at her. *"Huh?* What'd ya say? What am I supposed to do with your stinky shoe?"

"It's not stinky!" yelled Paige, which set her wobbling on the bar. "Whoa there!" she whispered, tightening her grip. Her hands were growing sweatier and clammier. If they slipped off the bar, down she'd go. Then Elwin would *really* feel something.

More kids had gathered below the monkey bars and were staring up at Paige. "Why don't you just flip and come down?" shouted Cynthia Sobkin.

Paige's eyebrows were sweating. "I'm not ready," she said.

"But recess is almost over!" called Sanjay.

Sure enough, Ms. Hardy-Wilson clapped her hands and shouted, "Room three—five minutes more!"

"Hey, Biloxi! Are you just going to hang there all day?" Viveca Frye pushed through the crowd. "Why don't you just flip over and climb down? Are you too scared?"

The words *too scared* were like an evil spell that squeezed even more sweat into Paige's hands. Any second now, she was going to slip off the bar and smash into a million pieces. If only someone would just give her a little push, she *knew* she could do it.

"Biloxi's in her socksies!" teased Viveca. "Lost her shoe, now what'll she do?"

Probably fall down dead on top of you, thought Paige. She shut her eyes and started to shake. The bars were shaking, too. Any moment now, it was going to happen. Paige Turner was going to be the first student at Guggenheim Elementary to die from falling off the monkey bars.

When she opened her eyes, she saw why the bars were shaking so hard. "Gavi!" When Gavi reached her, Paige whispered, "I'm stuck!"

Gavi bit her bottom lip and glanced down. "I know. So here's what we'll do: We'll pretend to chat, and then I'll get behind you and pretend to knock against your feet. That should give you plenty of oomph for flipping over. 'Kay?"

Paige nodded. "But tell me when you're gonna do it, all right? I need to be ready!"

"Will do," said Gavi calmly, and then in a voice loud

enough for the crowd below to hear, she said, "Hey, um, Oklahoma . . . you'd better come down now. The teacher's calling us! Move yer keester!"

Gavi inched herself behind Paige and in a stage whisper counted off: "One, two, three . . . go!" Gavi pushed the bottoms of Paige's feet, sending Paige clumsily flipping over the bar. *Clang!* The other clog flew off and banged against the bar below, leaving Paige shoeless. But when she opened her eyes, she had two feet on the bar and was facing her friend.

"Ain't that a dinger?" said Gavi with two thumbs up.

"It sure is!" said Paige, swabbing each leg of her jeans with a sweaty hand. "Thanks, Gavi. You're the best!"

"Room three, time to go in!" their teacher shouted. With trembling hands, trembling legs, and what felt like trembling eyeballs, Paige carefully climbed down. The minute her socks hit the rubber mat, a wave of relief swelled inside her. She stepped into her clogs, enjoying the indescribable pleasure of standing on solid ground.

"Next time wear sneakers," Elwin told her.

"Boy, Biloxi," said Viveca as she walked by, "you sure looked weird up there."

Paige swallowed hard, and the joyful wave of relief quickly turned to an undertow of embarrassment. Some of the other kids nearby began snickering. Paige tried to think of something to say to Viveca, but her voice disappeared, as if she'd been rejinxed.

"Don't pay attention to her," said Gavi. "You actually

flipped... all the way up there! You'd make a pretty good secret agent."

But Paige knew that if it hadn't been for Gavi, she'd still be stuck on the monkey bars, and would be the joke of the whole fourth grade. "C'mon, Oklahoma," said Gavi. "Let's head back to the ranch!" Gavi took off, galloping toward the open doors. But Paige didn't have any gallop in her. Instead, she dragged her feet as she clomped back inside, listening to the grit of the playground scraping the bottom of her shoes. *The sound,* thought Paige, *of a real Biloxi.*

Chapter Eight

The Milkshake Mess

One afternoon, after they'd copied down their Vivid Vocabulary words, Ms. Hardy-Wilson rounded up the class and led them to the annual school book fair. "Today you're just going to browse," she told them. "Check out the goods, and make a list of any books you'd like to buy."

The moment they stepped into the school library, room 3 erupted into a long chorus of *"Ooh!"* and *"Ahh!"* All the tables were pushed together and crowded with shiny new books. Some of the books even came with stuff attached. It reminded Paige of the junky prizes inside Corn Zappies.

Everyone crowded around the books that had CDs

or necklaces attached to their covers. "I wanna get that one!" they called. "I'm getting that one!"

Gavi rushed up to Paige with a book on Morse code. It came with a special box that made all the *dit-dit-dah* sounds when you pressed the lever. It cost twice as much as the other book on secret codes, but Gavi had an idea. "If we both bring in enough, we could pool our money," she told Paige. "Then we could share this book and learn how to send secret messages—just like real spies!" Paige agreed it was a great idea.

Gavi was practically shivering with excitement over the Morse code book. "You mean it?" she said.

"Sure," said Paige. "Morse code would be great to know if either one of us ever gets jinxed again." But a big Biloxi feeling still sat inside Paige, as if Viveca had cast another kind of spell on her. It was the kind that made her feel all shrunken up. So she wandered the book fair quietly, pretending to browse, though she actually felt very far away.

And then she saw it.

"Hey, look at this!" Paige cried. Tugging Gavi's sleeve, she pointed to a small cluster of toy monkeys hanging from a cardboard jungle scene. Paige loved the beige-and-creamy-white one. It had long, furry arms with Velcro hands that could stick together. Best of all, it was wearing a red cowboy hat.

"Oh, Gavi, isn't he just the best?" Paige sighed. "His fur reminds me of a delicious milkshake. And look—he has a red cowboy hat!" She pointed down at her shoes.

"It matches my clogs! Wouldn't he make the perfect sidekick?"

"I guess," said Gavi, shrugging. "Wonder how much he costs," said Paige, turning over the price tag. "Whoa! That's a lot!" Gavi peeked over her shoulder. "Actually, it costs the same as the Morse code book."

"Huh," said Paige, petting the monkey. She noticed a small booklet hanging from its arm. "Gavi, look! He even comes with a birth certificate! Maybe he even has his own Web page!"

Ms. Hardy-Wilson clapped her hands. "Room three, finish up your lists!"

For the rest of the day, Paige could think about nothing but the monkey with the red cowboy hat and his own birth certificate.

With a cute cowboy monkey sidekick, Paige would feel like a *real* Oklahoma. The only problem was Gavi.

Paige had promised to put all her money toward the Morse code book. But Oklahoma needed a sidekick.

The next day, room 3 returned to the library. Everyone had a shopping list and money. While Gavi ran to get the Morse code book, Paige wandered over to the monkey display. Elwin Diggins raced up and yanked down one of the monkeys. The moment he clasped the Velcro monkey hands around his neck, a deep, warm smile spread across his face.

Ms. Hardy-Wilson called out, "My class—make your purchases! We need to saddle up and head for the gym!"

Katie Bortznik suddenly came from behind and claimed a second monkey.

"Oh, Milkshake!" Paige whispered to the one remaining monkey. And without a second thought, she pulled him into her arms. His beige-and-creamy-white fur felt even silkier than it looked.

"Move!" boomed Viveca, pushing past Paige. Her arms could barely contain the three posters, large kaleidoscope, and two books with stuff attached that she was clutching.

Paige fastened the monkey's hands around her neck. Viveca wasn't going to get her monkey, too! With Milkshake's fluffy arms now hugging her, Paige felt as if she was floating to the front of the library—past Viveca, and past all the shiny new books. She dug into her pocket and quickly handed her teacher a ball of crumpled bills.

"Hey," said Gavi, coming up behind her. "I thought we were going to pool our money!" She held up the Morse code book with the special box that made the dit-dit-dah sounds. We can't buy this book if you get the monkey!"

Paige looked down as she stroked Milkshake's silky back. "I *have* to have him, Gavi. He makes me feel like a real Oklahoma." She looked up. "And we could have a special picnic at lunch—you, me, and Milkshake!"

"Forget it," said Gavi. "I'll get something else," she said, and turned away, placing the Morse code book down on the table as she went.

Later, at recess, Paige's classmates made a big fuss over Milkshake. Lily and Mack ran over from their class to admire him. But not Gavi. She stayed on the far side of the yard and played foursquare with some other kids.

"Now that you have a cowboy sidekick," said Sanjay, "you really do seem like an Oklahoma."

Paige beamed as she sat on a bench with Milkshake on her knee. As more kids gathered around, she took out her lucky rubber lightbulb and pretended it was a microphone and she was the host of her own talk show. "Welcome, everybody," she announced, "to the *Magic Lightbulb Show*! I'm so excited, because today we have a very special guest with us—Milkshake the Monkey!" The kids around Paige applauded. "Milkshake here has just wrapped up his ninth feature film, *Going Bananas!* and published the fourteenth book in his bestselling series, *The Mysterious*

The Magic Light Bulb Show

Monkey Tales. Tell us, Milkshake, with all your projects, when do you find time to just swing through the trees and, y'know, hang with friends?"

"Oh, isn't this perfect?" said Viveca, joining the crowd. "A monkey for a monkey!" Paige hid the rubber lightbulb in her lap, and her heart began to gallop. But when she looked around, the other kids weren't laughing along with Viveca.

"Milkshake, tell us more about your new movie!" said Lily.

Sanjay thrust a paper and pen in front of Paige. "Can I have Milkshake's autograph?"

"Oh, Milkshake," said Mack in a swoony, star-struck voice. "You're *so* lovable. I just dream of giving you a great big hug!" Paige laughed and, forgetting about Viveca, wrapped Milkshake's hands around Mack's neck. "I'll never wash my neck again!" sighed Mack.

Viveca stood by, watching. Her lips twitched. Her

nose sniffed up and down like a rabbit's. And then, in the teensiest, tinesiest voice ever, she said, "Can I hold him...Oklahoma?"

Paige wasn't sure she'd heard right. But one look at the other kids' faces and she knew Viveca had finally said it.

"Well...um...okay...I guess," said Paige. "For a little." She nodded to Mack to give Milkshake to Viveca. But the moment she did, Paige wanted him back.

"He's *so* soft," crooned Viveca, running her hand over Milkshake. It was the same hand that had zapped Paige with the personal jinx.

Paige turned to Lily and signaled with her eyes. "Lily, I think it's your turn now."

"Oh, yeah!" said Lily, getting the signal loud and clear.

"Hey, I know!" said Viveca, ignoring her. "We could have a Milkshake fan club!"

"That's a great idea!" said Cynthia Sobkin. "A club would be so cool!"

"I don't know," said Paige. Her stomach crumpled up like a failed spelling test. "That just seems kind of silly."

Viveca said, "Oh, not a whole club for a stuffed monkey! He could just be our mascot, and we could have meetings in my basement. We just got a Ping-Pong table, and we could hang out there. And my mom will make us *real* milkshakes!" Viveca tossed Milkshake back to Paige and grabbed Cynthia. "Let's make a list of everyone in the club," said Viveca, and marched away with Cynthia.

Paige felt as if she'd been spun around several times and then commanded to walk a straight line. Whenever she saw Gavi, Gavi turned and walked in the opposite direction with her lips pressed together, as if she was holding in a bad word.

Paige had to find a way to make Gavi understand why it was so important to have a sidekick. She ripped out a piece of notebook paper and began to write Gavi a note. But a strong scent of something candy-sweet distracted her. She looked up and Viveca was leaning toward her, holding out a smelly glitter marker. "Hey, Oklahoma," Viveca said. "Smell this one. It's chocolate-marshmallow kabob!"

Viveca was offering her a smelly marker? For a moment, Paige just gazed adoringly at it. Then she took the marker from Viveca's hand, uncapped it, and breathed in. "Wow!" she said. "I can practically taste it!"

Viveca nodded. "I know! That's my favorite, too. But you can use it for now."

"Really?"

"Sure!" So Paige made a few lines with the marker on her note to Gavi and inhaled them. *Mmm!* Her boring old lined paper had turned into a delicious treat! The lines she'd drawn smelled so good she wanted to lick them up.

"And later," said Viveca, "we can figure out a day for our first club meeting."

"Well, I don't really know about…well, um… maybe," said Paige. She looked down at her note to Gavi, now yummy but messy with squiggles of chocolate-marshmallow kabob. She couldn't use it for her note anymore. She decided she'd write another note later and folded the yummy paper into a fan to wave beneath her nose.

For the rest of the day, whenever Viveca came up to her with a smile and said "Howdy, Oklahoma!" or "Hey, Okey-doke!" Paige felt a rush of relief. It was happening. Viveca liked her! Which meant she wouldn't tease her anymore. All thanks to being Oklahoma.

Paige was so excited, she ran up to Gavi when the bell rang and said, "Howdy, pardner!"

"I think you must mean someone else," sniffed Gavi, and ran to catch up with Lily and Mack. Paige turned and saw Viveca with her usual trail of girls. But Viveca wasn't calling out to Paige to join them. *Well,* thought Paige, *maybe tomorrow.*

Chapter Nine
Paige Rage

Outside the Guggenheim School, the day was crisp and bright. The sidewalks were covered with crunchy leaves. It was the kind of day that usually filled Paige with a wonderful light, skippy feeling. But not today. Even with Milkshake bouncing against her chest as she walked, it felt as if something hard and prickly was pounding inside her. *Gavi's just jealous,* thought Paige. *She'll get used to Milkshake and we'll buy a Morse code book another time.*

When Paige reached her house, no one was home, and then she remembered: it was Thursday. Conrad had lacrosse practice on Thursdays, and her parents worked till five. And on Thursdays, Paige was supposed to go home with Gavi and wait for her mom to pick her up. *Ugh!* She set her backpack down on the front steps and searched the outside pouch for her emergency house key. She felt all around for it, but it wasn't there. She unzipped the main compartment of her backpack. Her hands wiggled deep down beneath her books, around her rubber lightbulb, and in between all the papers stuffed inside.

No key.

But she couldn't go to Gavi's. Gavi would probably say "I think you mean some other house" and slam the door in her face.

Paige turned her backpack upside down and shook everything out. Still no key. A breeze scuttled her papers over the leaves blanketing the yard, and Paige leapt about, gathering them up. But the moment she set them down and turned her back to search her pockets for her key, a strong wind swooped down, tumbling the papers across the yard. One of them was Milkshake's birth certificate.

"Nooo!" Paige called, chasing after it. *"Wait! Stop!"* she shouted as if it was a runaway dog. Just as the certificate flew down to the curb, a strong gust scooped it up and slammed it down in the middle of the street. Cars zoomed by while Paige stood with the tips of her clogs over the edge of the curb.

When the way was finally clear, she dashed out and grabbed the paper.

Saved!

But the certificate had landed facedown. When Paige

turned it over and saw that its pale yellow surface was smudged with road dirt, she squatted down to brush some of it off. As she stood up, a car suddenly screeched to a stop. The car looked enormous, and a voice inside Paige started shouting, *Run! Run back to the curb!* But she couldn't move. Her whole self was frozen in the middle of the street. The voice inside pleaded, *Somebody push me back to the sidewalk!* But no one was there to give her the push, and she stood there until the sharp blare of the car's horn sent her scurrying back to the curb.

As the car rolled by, the driver scowled at Paige. She was trembling. What if the car had run her over? Her parents would've absolutely killed her!

She watched a few more cars go by and then scrambled around the front yard snatching up her papers, her knees still full of jumping beans. When she'd finally collected everything, she plopped down on the front steps and examined Milkshake's birth certificate. It still had dirty street smudges and a bad crease on one side. She smoothed it out as best she could and took out her social studies book. It was her heaviest book, so she stuck the certificate in a chapter on the Midwest and slammed it shut. Hopefully, a little time in Omaha would smooth things out.

Paige then took out her Vivid Vocabulary list. Her teacher loved words and encouraged the class to use Vivid Vocabulary in their writing. "Vivid words," she told her class, "produce powerful feelings and strong pictures in the mind." This week's list sure did that. The list had words such as *scorching, prickly, nauseating, croaking, slithering,* and Paige's favorite, *putrid.* But it was hard to concentrate on Vivid Vocabulary. A chilling wind kept scruffling the pages of her workbook, and the cold air made the fine hair on her arms tingle. On top of that, every time she heard a car, Paige's head bopped up to see if it was one of her parents.

Finally, after about a thousand years, Mrs. Turner's car pulled into the driveway. The car door slammed and Paige's mother strode up the path, her face pulled tight. "What are you doing here?" she asked Paige.

Paige looked about. Wasn't this her house? Of course it was. "I went to Gavi's," continued her mother, "and when I asked her where you were, she said you didn't walk home with her. She acted as if she had no idea why you wouldn't have gone home with her. And I certainly don't know why, either!" Mrs. Turner's voice was high, and it wobbled between anger and worry. Definitely more toward anger. She took a deep breath, stomped up the front steps, and shook out her keys.

Inside, Mrs. Turner set down her bag with a loud, annoyed *thunk* and turned to Paige. "So why didn't you walk home with Gavi? I was very worried about you!"

If she was so worried, why was she so mean and growly? Paige's throat cramped and her eyes filled with tears. "Well, I was worried, too!" she said, sniffling into Milkshake's head. She wondered if she should tell her mother she was mostly crying because she'd almost been hit by a car. She decided not to. "I forgot to go to Gavi's, and then I couldn't find my house key."

"You *forgot* to go to Gavi's?" At least her mother's voice was moving away from anger and more toward worry. "How could you forget that? You *always* go to Gavi's on Thursdays."

Paige lifted Milkshake's tail. "Because of this," she said, and let the tail drop.

"You forgot because of a stuffed monkey?"

"He's not just a monkey. He's my sidekick. His name is Milkshake. And Gavi got mad when I bought him at the book fair." She nuzzled her nose into Milkshake's cowboy hat.

"Wait a minute. I thought we gave you money to buy *books* at the book fair," said Mrs. Turner.

"Well, I almost bought a book on Morse code," said Paige, looking up. "Gavi wanted us to buy it together. But I needed Milkshake more!"

"Needed?"

"Wanted," muttered Paige. "But, Mom, he's the perfect trusty sidekick. He even has a little red cowboy hat! And Gavi knows that! But she got mad at me anyway."

Mrs. Turner fingered the hat and nodded. "Hmm... well, he is pretty cute." Paige followed her mother into the dining room, where she stopped in front of a tall, narrow bookcase filled with teapots. Mrs. Turner had a large collection of teapots, and today she chose the one with the handle and spout that looked like delicate tree branches.

She carried it into the kitchen and put the kettle on to boil. "Y'know," said Mrs. Turner in a calmer, tea-making voice, "I can see why Gavi got angry with you. Maybe you've given her the idea that being Oklahoma is more important than being her friend."

Paige swallowed hard and clutched Milkshake to her chest. "That's not true!" she shouted. "That's not true at all!" Her voice was wobbly, and she didn't want to start crying. That would be such an un-Oklahoma-ish thing to do. But she couldn't keep the crying Paige part from pushing through, so she stormed out of the kitchen and went straight to the living room.

As soon as she sat down at the piano, Paige yanked Milkshake off her neck and flung him across the room. She barely missed knocking over a lamp. Then she slammed down some scales, which led right into pounding chords of rage. It felt good. No, it felt *great* to be loud and sad and mad at everything and everyone. Her fingers had never worked so hard, and through the crashing chords, her brooding thoughts stomped along:

It could've been a perfect day. Paige's fingers skipped along the high, plinky notes: *ba-dink, ba-dink, ba-dink!*

But then it turned horrible! Paige's fingers scurried down the keyboard to pounce on the low, sulking keys.

She had tried to have individual flair—she went back to the high, plinky notes: *fwip, fwip, fwip!* And discover one of her many selves, just the way her teacher had said—*fwip, fwip, fwip!*

Having Milkshake made her feel more like an Oklahoma. Here Paige's fingers galloped out some cowboyish chords. *Ta-da-ta-da-ta-da!*

But then Gavi got mad—*wham!*

So Paige forgot to walk home with her—*thwop!*

And then her crabtree mother yelled at her—*fwomp!*

And now everything was putrid, putrid, putrid! At this part, Paige's fingers went crazy. She clenched her fingers into a fist and pounded the black keys. Then she spread her fingers wide and slammed on the white. Pound, *SLAM!* Pound, *SLAM!* Pound, *SLAM!*

"That doesn't sound like your *usual* lesson!" Mrs. Turner shouted from the kitchen. Paige stopped. The sound of her mother's voice had broken the creative trance, and Paige slumped at the piano, exhausted. Her elbows collapsed by her sides, and she took a lot of slow, deep cleansing breaths. In through the nose, out through the mouth. She wiped the tears from her cheeks and then wiped her hands dry on her pants.

For the final movement of "Paige Rage" (the title had come to her while she was knuckling the black keys), Paige hunched over the keyboard and played a slow, mournful tune, as sad as any Russian piece Mrs. Klonsky had ever taught her. And the words in her head went like this:

How can I discover one of my many selves
When no one,
And I mean no one,
When nobody, nobody, nobody, not even one little,
stupid person,
Will ever let me try?
Oh, prickling, scorching, nauseating, croaking,
Putrid, slithering...DIE!

"Paige Rage" ended in a very loud, somber chord. It was deeply satisfying, and for the moment, Paige felt really, really good.

Chapter Ten

Project Oklahoma

Paige's foul mood was still with her at breakfast when Conrad poured the last good bowl of Corn Zappies, leaving Paige with mostly orange-colored Zappie dust.

Her mood got even worse when Mrs. Turner bounced into the kitchen and said, "Guess who's coming to visit us all the way from California!"

"Aunt Joni?" said Conrad, as if his mother had just asked for the sum of one plus one.

"Not just Aunt Joni," Mrs. Turner said, pouring herself a cup of tea. She tugged the page with the crossword puzzle out from beneath the comics Mr. Turner was reading. "Your cousin, Cordelia!"

Paige had finished up the few measly cereal nuggets

Conrad had left her and was deciding whether she should get a straw to sip up the orange-colored milk. But now she felt as if she couldn't even slurp up a mouthful of air. "Really?...Cordelia?...*Here?*"

"Yep. Aunt Joni has a convention in New York, so she figured she'd bring Cordelia with her! They'll stay with us for the weekend and then take the train down to New York City and stay the rest of the time with Grandma."

Conrad groaned. "Ugh, not Cordelia!"

"She's your cousin," scolded Mrs. Turner.

"And a real pain in the...patootie," said Conrad.

"Mmm," agreed Mr. Turner without looking up from the paper.

Paige didn't feel ready for Cordelia. Not yet. Project Oklahoma still wasn't complete. But then, maybe having Cordelia around could help Paige put the finishing touches on her new self. And then maybe Gavi would see that Milkshake really *had* helped Paige become Oklahoma!

At school, Paige wore Milkshake around her neck, which made her feel a little better, although Gavi still ignored her. After lunch, Ms. Hardy-Wilson told the class to hush up for an important announcement. Standing by her desk with a yellow paper in her hand, their teacher said, "I'm thrilled to tell y'all that a special event is coming up—the annual Fourth-Grade Fall Variety Show!" Room 3 rumbled with excitement, but Paige sat very still. Memories of last year's Poetry Slam filled her stomach with squirmy snakes.

"'All students are encouraged to participate,'" read Ms. Hardy-Wilson. "And this year, the money for the tickets goes toward a new playground."

Everyone cheered.

"I'm sure this class is just bursting with talent, so I hope lots of you will sign up. The more people who perform, the more tickets we'll sell. I've put the sheet here on this easel so you can write down your names and the kind of act you'll perform."

Viveca leaned over toward Paige. "Hey, Okey-doke, you gonna help with refreshments?" Paige squinted at her and Viveca's face went soft. "I mean, because of your stage fright."

Paige thought of Cordelia turning cartwheels across a stage. She sucked in her breath and let it out noisily through her nose. "Actually," said Paige, "I haven't decided yet."

"Oh," said Viveca. "Hey, I know! We could do an act together."

Viveca wanted to do an act...with her? "What kind of an act?" Paige asked.

"Oh, y'know—a dance! Like a cowgirl dance. Maybe we could even include Milkshake!"

Paige clapped a hand over Milkshake. "I don't know about that," she said. "I don't really dance."

"That's okay," chirped Viveca. "I do. I've taken tap since I was four. And we could figure out something for you to do. Like, maybe you could gallop around me while I do a cowgirl tap dance. Maybe I could even twirl a lasso!"

A vision of Paige galloping around Viveca while she danced with Milkshake set twenty billion alarms clanging inside Paige's body. It was as if Viveca was trying to be Oklahoma, too! "I don't know," Paige muttered. If only she'd stayed her plain old self.

"Well, it's a really good idea," said Viveca. "And honestly, what else would you do?"

Viveca's question filled Paige with a jinxy feeling. She stretched her legs out, and as she looked down at her clogs she thought about Cordelia and how she'd inspired Paige to be gutsier. "Well," said Paige, "I play the pia—"

Viveca's brows shot up in a scalding dare, a look that quickly sucked all the Oklahoma out of Paige. "Um, I have to think about it," Paige said, pulling her legs back in and ducking her head inside her desk.

As she scrambled through her things, half searching, half hiding, she found a paper fortune-teller Gavi had made for her long before the Milkshake mess. She took it out and picked the drawing of the moon on one corner. Pinching the fortune-teller up and out, Paige spelled *M-O-O-N*. Then she picked the number eight—the month of her birthday: *1-2-3-4-5-6-7-8*, she counted silently. And then another number, *26*—the day of her birthday. It took a long time to count that one out. But finally, she opened up the fortune-teller and read: *You are a true friend.*

Her elbows sagged. The real fortune, she knew,

should've been *You are turning into Viveca's monkey.* And turning into Viveca's monkey was *not* what being Oklahoma was supposed to feel like.

Cor-*delia!* The way Aunt Joni said her daughter's name made Paige think of someone stomping on the brakes of a car. But Cousin Cordelia didn't come with brakes. In fact, she entered the Turner house like a runaway shopping cart rattling down a steep hill.

Cordelia was almost a year younger than Paige, but in the same grade. When Cordelia told her, "I just made the cutoff," Paige had imagined her cousin skidding under some heavy garage door seconds before it slammed down to bar all the other kids from cramming their way into kindergarten. Cordelia was still as small and wiry as Paige remembered, with two wavy blond ponytails, and teeth like little pieces of gum. The backpack she wore was a wondrous thing, with lanyards, whistles, beads, an army of rubber figures attached, and a gazillion key chains, too. Whenever Cordelia hunched it up or swung it down to the floor, as she was doing now, it made a wonderful tinkling, jangly sound. It made her sound as if she belonged to some exciting, exotic tribe.

Without her backpack weighing her down, Cordelia now bounced more than walked. "I'll teach you the new poem I learned!" she whispered to Paige. And from the way Cordelia's face lit up, Paige knew it wasn't the kind of poem she'd want to recite in front of her parents.

"I can almost do a cartwheel!" Paige told her. "I'll show you!"

But Cordelia had already sprung from the front hall to the kitchen. "Fantastic!" she said, eyeing the narrow doorway between the kitchen and the family room. Cordelia ran to the doorway and, in a blink, filled the space like an oversized insect. Her fingers were splayed and the soles of her sneakers were pressed flat against the sides of the doorway two feet off the ground. "Watch this!" she said. "I can climb and recite poetry at the same time!" Inching her way up the doorway, Cordelia chanted in a boisterous playground voice:

A fart is a noisy eruption,
It lives in the city of Bum.
It plays in the valley of Trouser Leg,
And erupts with a musical hum!

By the end of her "poem," Cordelia's head pressed against the top of the doorway.

Wow! thought Paige.

Mrs. Turner was also amazed, but not in the same way. The moment Paige's mother and Aunt Joni entered the kitchen and caught sight of Cordelia, the human insect, Mrs. Turner's eyes bugged out. But Aunt Joni's face was calm, as if climbing the walls while reciting fart poetry was an everyday occurrence. "Cor-*delia*," said Aunt Joni. "You know you shouldn't climb walls with your shoes on."

Paige and her mother shared a look.

That's it?

"Okay, coming down!" yelled Cordelia. Her face scrunched tightly with the concentration of an expert rock climber, and the moment her feet hit the floor she announced that she needed a drink.

Mrs. Turner said, "Oh, well…let's see what we have," and once again shot Aunt Joni a significant look. Paige knew her mother was waiting for her aunt to say something like "Cor-*delia*, did you forget to unpack your manners?" But she didn't. Paige found it weirdly thrilling.

"How about some lemonade?" asked Mrs. Turner, reaching into the refrigerator.

"Is it pink?"

Paige's mother turned around, holding the pitcher. "It's yellow," she said. "Like lemons."

"Oh." Cordelia already seemed disappointed with the Turner household. "Can I have a straw? I always drink my drinks with a straw."

Mrs. Turner smiled stiffly and said, "Sure thing." She got a straw from the cabinet and plunked it into Cordelia's lemonade, but Cordelia didn't say "Thank you." Aunt Joni didn't remind Cordelia to say it, but Paige's mother kept on smiling. It was a totally fake smile. And by the time all the lemonade was sucked up noisily through the straw and all the fingerprints and shoe scuffs in the doorway were wiped off, Mrs. Turner's smile had gone from totally fake to super-fake.

She was still sporting her super-fake smile when she unwrapped the gift from Aunt Joni. "Oh, a teapot!" chirped Mrs. Turner, in a super-fake cheery voice.

"For your collection," said Aunt Joni. "Cordelia picked it out all by herself!" Aunt Joni smiled admiringly at Cordelia. The teapot was blue, with lily pads painted all around, which wasn't so bad. But the knob on the top was shaped like an ugly squatting frog, its long tongue stretched out with a fly stuck at the tip. The handle was also shaped like a frog, but with its legs splayed wide as if it was hopping in some weird stretched-out way.

"Isn't that *special*!" said Mrs. Turner. "I don't think I have anything quite like this!" In her whole, entire life, Paige had never seen her mother act so incredibly fake. "I'll have to move a few things in my collection to make room for it. But for now, let's just put it here!" Paige's mother went to the dining room and a set the teapot on a small side table. "There," she said. "Doesn't that look nice?"

Her mother's fakeness had grown unbearable, so Paige said to Cordelia, "Let's go to my room." But once they were upstairs, Cordelia turned toward Conrad's room instead. She said she wanted to snoop around and look for Incriminating Evidence.

"I don't think we should," said Paige. The thought of spying on Conrad made her think of Gavi. But that was different. Gavi was interested in spying on *Conrad,* not going through his stuff.

"Oh, come on," said Cordelia. "We can find out his most abominable secrets!"

Paige crossed the threshold into Conrad's room, but with Cordelia there, it didn't feel right. Her cousin hadn't spent enough time in their house to be uncovering Conrad's secrets. "Let's do something else," suggested Paige.

"What, you've never looked through your brother's stuff?"

"Of course I have. But he's *my* brother."

"Weirdsville," said Cordelia, and began opening Conrad's desk drawers. It didn't take her long to find something. "Ooh, look! A note!"

"Don't!" cried Paige, but Cordelia ignored her. Even when Paige dashed over to slam the drawer shut, her cousin didn't move her fingers.

"Ouchie! Ouchie!" Cordelia shouted, hopping around like a cartoon character. She blew on her fingers as if they were on fire but still held on to the note. When she finally stopped hopping, Cordelia unfolded the note and read: "'Maeve Wits—'" Paige glanced anxiously toward the door. She hoped her brother wouldn't catch them. "Wits...shonski?...Maeve Witshonski?...Ooh! It even has her *phone* number!" Cordelia flashed her teeny little chewing-gum teeth. "Conrad has a girlfriend!"

Paige scowled, partly in disbelief and partly because she was miffed that Cordelia had unearthed Incriminating Evidence so quickly. It had taken Paige years to discover that Conrad was afraid of the dark. But discovering a truly abominable secret, like a girlfriend? In under five minutes? It just wasn't fair.

"Let's get out of here," said Paige. She plucked the note from Cordelia's hand and shoved it into the drawer.

In Paige's room, her cousin settled down enough to teach Paige a fun new card game that involved a lot of slapping cards. But as soon as Cordelia spied Milkshake hiding behind a pillow on Paige's bed, she jumped up and grabbed him and fastened his paws around her neck.

Paige's heart began to race. "Um, he's kind of special to me," she said. "So could you please put him back?" Cordelia acted as if she hadn't heard Paige and kept dealing the cards. Paige thought back to her visit to Berkeley, when she had wanted to be the banker in Monopoly and Cordelia had insisted that *she* was always the banker. "*My* house, *my* rules," Cordelia had told her.

Now that Cordelia was at Paige's house, it would

work the other way around. "*My* house," said Paige, leaning toward Cordelia. "So you know—"

As Paige reached for Milkshake, Cordelia leaned way back and said, "But *I'm* the guest."

For a moment Paige was speechless, and a vision of Viveca flashed through her mind. How could she have missed what a brat Cordelia could be? Maybe it had something to do with the time difference. Maybe when Paige visited Cordelia in Berkeley, her brain had been jet-lagged.

But Paige wasn't in Berkeley now. She was in her own time zone and in her own room. So with all her might, she pushed her Oklahoma self forward and said, "You might be the guest... but *my* room, *my* stuff." She looked Cordelia right in the eye and didn't blink.

Cordelia frowned, but in a snap, she shrugged off the comment and yanked Milkshake from her neck. "Weirdsville," she muttered, tossing him back to Paige.

With Milkshake's hands clasped firmly around her neck, Paige scooped up the cards. "This time," she told her cousin, "I'm the dealer."

Chapter Eleven

The Cordelia Calamity

"Guess who!" Cordelia sang out when Conrad came home from lacrosse practice. She'd snuck up behind him and covered his eyes with her hands.

"Oh, geez, you're really here, huh?" said Conrad, peeling Cordelia's hands off his face. "So how's life in Berserkely?" Cordelia laughed and told Paige she was lucky to have a brother.

As Conrad put his equipment away, Cordelia kept peppering him with questions. "Can I try out your lacrosse stick?" "Can we hang out in your room?" "Do you have a girlfriend?" She winked at Paige.

Conrad gave an emphatic "No" to all of her questions,

and Cordelia followed him into the kitchen, where he said hello to Aunt Joni.

"Don't fill up on bread," Mrs. Turner warned as he grabbed a bagel and headed upstairs. "We're having supper soon!"

The girls followed Conrad, with Paige dragging behind. At the top of the steps, Cordelia said, "Bet I can guess your girlfriend's initials!"

Conrad whipped around so fast Cordelia and Paige nearly tumbled backward down the stairs. "Bet you need to find something else to do," he said, and went to his room.

But Cordelia followed him, and before he could shut the door on her, she'd pushed her way into his room and plopped down into his beanbag chair. "Are your girlfriend's initials . . . *M.W.*?"

Conrad glared at Paige, who hadn't ventured farther than the doorway. "Speaking of names," he said, "have you told her yet?"

"No—not doing that," said Paige, shaking her head and glaring at her brother.

Cordelia sat up straight in the beanbag chair. "Told me what?"

"She has a new name," said Conrad. "It's—"

"Never mind!" said Paige sternly, and shot Conrad a look that said *Don't you dare.* For some reason, telling Cordelia about Oklahoma felt like handing over Incriminating Evidence.

"—*Oklahoma!*" crowed Conrad.

"Con*rat!*"

Cordelia looked astonished. "As in the forty-sixth state, with more man-made lakes than any other?"

For a moment, Paige looked at her cousin, speechless. Then, leaning against the door, she folded her arms and turned her attention back to Conrad. "So...speaking of names, who's Maeve Witshonski?"

"*What?*" squealed Conrad. "How do you know that name?"

"That's for *us* to know and *you* to never find out," sang Cordelia, sinking deeper into the beanbag chair. "Is she your girlfriend?"

"Ick, no! I'm just doing a science project with her!" But his freckles were blushing. "Besides, it's none of your business." Conrad threw Paige a Cottage Cheese Monster look.

Paige ignored him. "Oh, I just remembered something," she said lightly, and left the room, closing the door behind her. *Let Conrad be stuck with Cordelia for a while,* she thought, and went downstairs, settling herself on the bottom step, where she could listen in on her mother and Aunt Joni in the kitchen. Their voices rose and dipped like notes of music, laughing and whispering. Again, Paige thought of Gavi, and how they would spy on their mothers talking on the phone and laugh about how their parents must've come from the planet Boring.

After a few minutes of mother babble, Paige heard the bathroom door slam shut. No doubt Conrad was hiding from Cordelia. It occurred to Paige then that she should write a piece of music about Cordelia's visit. The loud, banging notes would be Cordelia bouncing around the house. And the high, plinkety ones would be her mother's fake cheery smile. Paige's composition would be a rhapsody, and she would call it "The Cordelia Calamity."

After supper, Paige and Cordelia watched a movie and played two rounds of Life. By ten o'clock, Paige was yawning. "Time to hit the hay," said Mr. Turner, and Paige was grateful for her father's announcement.

"I'm not tired!" said Cordelia. "I'm on West Coast time." Mr. and Mrs. Turner exchanged a look.

"Oh, I hope you don't mind," said Aunt Joni. "We'll just stay up till we're ready for bed." Paige didn't want to go to bed first and look like a baby in front of her cousin. But after a while, it was hard to keep her eyes open.

"You're on East Coast time," her mother said. "Up you go." Happily, Paige slid off the sofa and dragged herself up to bed.

In the morning, Paige tiptoed around the lump of her cousin in the sleeping bag on the floor and went downstairs. Aunt Joni was at the kitchen table, sipping coffee, and Paige was glad for a little time alone with her aunt.

Aunt Joni wore long feather earrings and a scarf in several shades of blue that draped so perfectly around her neck, it looked like ripples in a pond.

"So, Paige," said Aunt Joni. "Tell me about being Oklahoma." Paige dabbed her piece of French toast three times in the syrup. She needed time to figure out what to say. She couldn't tell her aunt that she'd wanted to be more like Cousin Cordelia. Not just because it would be too embarrassing, but because she had changed her mind. She really *didn't* want to be like Cordelia. At least, not in every way.

Paige stabbed another spongy piece of French toast with her fork and said, "Being Oklahoma is kind of a school project. My teacher says we all have many selves inside." Quoting her teacher made Paige's cheeks flush, as if she'd let out a secret.

"You have a smart teacher," replied Aunt Joni, waving away her sister's offer of more coffee. "So what's your Oklahoma self like?" She looked eagerly at Paige. It made Paige squirm. The answer used to feel so clear. But now she wasn't sure. She knew it didn't mean acting like the whole world was your bouncy house, like Cordelia. But it was about being a *little* like Cordelia. And maybe it was a little bit of something else.

"Hey, who drank all the OJ?" Conrad had lumbered in and stood at the refrigerator, his eyes crusty with sleep. He shook the almost-empty orange juice carton accusingly at Paige.

"Wasn't me," said Paige, and gratefully launched into a fake argument with her brother over the nearly empty carton of juice.

By Sunday, it felt as if Cordelia had been visiting for a month. Everyone in the Turner family was exhausted and had spent a good deal of time either hiding in the bathroom, dashing out for "just a few errands," or suddenly remembering an emergency lacrosse practice.

While her mother rinsed the tea cups and got ready to take Aunt Joni and Cordelia to the train, Paige and her cousin sat at the piano. First they played some goofy songs together, like "Knuckles" and "Chopsticks." Then Paige played part of a sad, serious Mrs. Klonsky song. "Wow, you're really good!" said Cordelia.

"Thanks," said Paige.

"Now watch me!" Cordelia said, jumping up from the piano. She dipped herself down into a perfect handstand and walked on her hands around the living room. "Hey, I'm thirsty," she said, still upside down. So Paige followed her cousin as she cartwheeled from the living room to the front hallway. Cordelia's legs windmilled through the rooms in a rhythm Paige found enchanting. But after one rotation in the dining room, the tip of Cordelia's left sneaker hit the side table. There was a loud, porcelain-shattering crash, followed by Mrs. Turner and Aunt Joni swooping into the dining room.

"Whoops!" said Cordelia, now upright and staring down at the pieces of shattered teapot.

"Cor-*delia*!" exclaimed Aunt Joni.

"Oh, dear," said Mrs. Turner, bending down to pick up a large chipped frog leg.

"What can I say?" Aunt Joni said, looking down at her sister. "Cordelia's a very kinetic child. She needs to move around a lot."

Mrs. Turner looked up at her sister. "Spare me, Joni," she said, shaking the single frog leg at her. "Doing cartwheels in the house has nothing to do with being 'kinetic.' It's just *wrong*."

Aunt Joni's mouth hung open as if she'd been personal-jinxed. She squatted down to join Paige's mother in picking up the pieces of the teapot, and when she found her voice she said, "Of course we'll replace the teapot."

"Oh, no!" Mrs. Turner quickly replied. "*Really.* You don't have to. I have so many already. I wouldn't know where to put another one." Catching each other's eye, Paige and Mrs. Turner shared an invisible smile. Then, noticing the frog tongue with the tiny fly on the tip lying under the dining room table, Paige dropped to her knees and crawled over to it. She thought it might have magical powers, so she quietly stuck it in her pocket.

After all the bits of broken frog pot had been gathered and swept into the dustpan, Mrs. Turner dumped them into the kitchen trash. The shards of teapot crashing against one another made Aunt Joni wince. Cordelia looked away. But from the brightness in her mother's face when she returned, Paige understood that the sound had been music to her mother's ears. A strange kind of music, for sure, but it would make the perfect finale to "The Cordelia Calamity."

Chapter Twelve

Taking Joy

"Oklahoma! C'mere!" Paige wandered over to Viveca in the school yard. They were waiting for the bell to ring, and Viveca was surrounded by a small knot of kids. When Paige pushed in closer, she saw the paper and pen in Viveca's hands. "We've decided who's going to be in the Milkshake Club," Viveca told her, and Paige squatted down to read the list. "What about Gavi?" said Paige. Even though Paige wasn't crazy about the idea of a club headed up by Viveca, if Gavi was in the club, maybe she'd stop being mad at Paige.

Viveca shook her head. "Gavi's not in."

"Why not?"

"You know," said Viveca. She pinched her fingers on

either side of her head and pantomimed someone adjusting their glasses. Then, squeezing her voice in an imitation of Gavi, she said, "Oh, Viveca, can you tell us what *page* we're on?"

Paige drew back. Viveca was still mad at Gavi for unjinxing her? Paige turned away from the group and noticed Gavi passing by. Had she heard Viveca making fun of her? One look at her face and Paige knew the answer.

Turning back to Viveca, Paige said sternly, "If Gavi's not in the club, I don't want to be in it, either! Besides, who ever heard of a club about milkshakes?" The other kids looked from Paige to Viveca. Viveca's mouth puckered up tightly as if she was preparing to shoot Paige a real zinger. But it was also quivering a bit. Paige walked away to find Gavi. But she had already disappeared.

After school, Mr. Turner came home early so that someone would be there for Paige's weekly piano lesson with Mrs. Klonsky. Mrs. Klonsky always sat on Paige's left, which meant Paige always had a good view of the large mole close to her nose. It was so large and plump it seemed to Paige like a whole little planet. In her thick Russian accent, Mrs. Klonsky reminded Paige to always sit straight and bend her elbows out like little chicken wings.

Paige sat up straight at the piano. She bent her arms out like chicken wings and began her warm-up scales.

Usually, her fingers raced up and down the keys. But today, her fingers tripped and stumbled as if each one was blindfolded.

"Today your fingers are *stoopid,*" said Mrs. Klonsky. "You must teach them to be smart—like you." So Paige tried to teach her fingers. But the more she played, the more her fingers bumped into the black keys and slipped off the white.

Mrs. Klonsky placed her hands over Paige's. "Please stop," she said. "This is no good. Is there something sitting in your head?"

Paige stared down at her hands.

"Tell me," said Mrs. Klonsky.

Paige took a cleansing breath and quickly said, "In two weeks, the fourth grade is having this variety show. And I know I should play, but…"

"I see," said Ms. Klonsky. "You're telling me you are afraid to perform?"

Paige nodded. She tried digging down to her deepest, most Oklahoma-ish way of thinking. But the plain truth was she was too scared. Conrad was right. She was just a scared little mouse, not even the tiniest bit like Cousin Cordelia.

"You enjoy playing for yourself and for me, no?" asked Mrs. Klonsky.

Paige nodded.

"And you've played before in recitals. You cannot let your fear keep you from doing what you enjoy."

"But recitals are just for a few parents," said Paige. "Not a whole cafeteria full of people...and teachers. Why do I have to do it?"

"You don't," said Mrs. Klonsky. "It is just nice to share your...what is the word...pleasure?"

"Mm-hmm," Paige replied quietly.

"You should share your pleasure. When you do, the audience thanks you. And this will give you more courage."

Paige sat up and looked at Mrs. Klonsky. Courage was something she definitely wanted. But how could performing give her more courage? "What if I make a mistake?" she asked.

Mrs. Klonsky shrugged and said, "Eh! You play on. Art is full of mistakes. Like life. But we don't stop. We go on. And learn from our mistakes."

"But...what if I get so nervous I throw up all over the piano?"

As Mrs. Klonsky grimaced, the mole seemed to grow a little plumper. Paige imagined all the little people on Planet Mole bumping into one another. "This will not happen," said Mrs. Klonsky, shaking her head. "You will practice hard. And when you practice hard—even when you make mistake—you take joy. And when you take joy, you don't throw up. Now sit up straight," she said, tapping Paige lightly in the middle of her back, "and play for me again this passage. This time, no mistakes." She tapped Paige's elbow. Paige sat up straight, spread her chicken wings, and played the passage without any mistakes.

After her piano lesson, Paige sat down at the dining room table to do her homework. Her father was busy in the kitchen making chicken Caesar salad for supper. He knew Paige didn't like Caesar salad, but he'd made a deal with her. If she would try it again, he'd put hardly any dressing on her portion. Paige had agreed to the deal. She was determined to become less picky. And at least her father always served the salad along with a steamy baked potato and butter. A baked potato with butter could make almost anything tolerable.

Paige opened her notebook and took out her Vivid Vocabulary. She liked to start with the easy homework first. This week's list included words like *pandemonium, luscious, vibrant, enthusiastic, slosh, mammoth,* and *lurk*. The words filled Paige with a good feeling, and she thought about what Mrs. Klonsky had said. The important thing about mistakes was to move past them and keep going. She knew she'd made a big mistake—a *mammoth* mistake—thinking she had to become a completely different person overnight. People weren't like caterpillars in their cocoons. They didn't change all at once. It was more of a little-by-little kind of thing.

After looking up the definition of each word, Paige wrote her sentences:

There was great pandemonium when the monkey came to school. She took a look at the second word and wrote: *The brownies my friend shared were luscious.* And then: *Her new glasses are a vibrant red.* And then: *She is very enthusiastic about spying.*

The pen drooped in her fingers. If only getting Gavi back was as easy as writing out sentences. She thought how Gavi was always there to give her the extra push she needed to feel more like an Oklahoma. And how Gavi had always liked Paige—with extra guts or just regular.

Letting out a big, cleansing breath, Paige tried to think of a way to let Gavi know she'd made a mammoth mistake. She looked down at her sentences, and the last one she'd written turned suddenly from a sentence into an idea.

Paige ran upstairs, her mind racing—racing so fast she nearly crashed into Conrad on his way to the bathroom. His hands were covered with glue, and when he waved them close to Paige's face, she jumped back with a loud squeal.

"Hey, Oklahoma," said Conrad. "Wanna see my project on maggots? It's really gross."

"No. And don't call me that."

"I didn't call you gross—"

"Not that," said Paige.

"Oh...maggot? But I didn't call you maggot—"

"Not that, either!"

"Oh. I called you Okla—"

"I know what you called me! So don't call me that, *okay?*"

"Okay! Geez. So what, now you're Nevada?"

"No!" Paige stomped by her brother, but he followed her into her room. "Leave me alone, Conrad! There's something I need to do."

Ignoring her, Conrad said, "Did you know that flies lay about six hundred eggs in their lifetime? And that they lay them on stuff like garbage and dog poop? It's totally disgusting. Come to my room and I'll show you!"

But Paige shoved Conrad out of her room and slammed her door. She had an important project to work on. And it didn't involve a single maggot.

Chapter Thirteen

Spelling It Out

On Monday morning, Paige Turner's clogs clomped extra loudly on the way to her classroom. She took something out of her backpack and quickly stashed it inside her desk before anyone could see.

"Hey, Oklahoma, guess what?" Viveca said as they took out their owls and earthworms projects. "I've got a whole dance number worked up for the variety show. We can practice during recess."

Across the room, Gavi was working on her project with Katie Bortznik. They were laughing together.

"I can draw you a picture of the costume I'm going to wear," said Viveca. "Okey-doke, are you even listening to me?"

"Don't call me that."

"What?"

"Okey ... I mean, Oklahoma."

"But I thought you—"

"Never mind," said Paige, staring across the room at Gavi.

"Well, whatever your name is," said Viveca, "meet me at recess to practice our dance. I'll be by the jungle gym."

Paige nodded, but there was no way she was going to meet Viveca at recess or practice any kind of dance with her. Maybe doing a dance was Viveca's pleasure, as Mrs. Klonsky would say. But it sure wasn't Paige's. She had to move her keester and figure a way out of it.

At lunchtime, Viveca insisted that Paige eat with her so that they could discuss their performance. Viveca's idea of discussing it, however, was to talk about her "amazing costume" and the "great music" she and Milkshake would dance to. Viveca took out her marker that smelled like a pineapple-coconut smoothie and drew the costume she was going to wear. Paige had to admit, Viveca really knew how to draw. "You're a really good artist," she told her.

Viveca's nose twitched. "I'd like to design costumes for shows," she told Paige. "But my mother says I'll starve."

"I think your mother's wrong."

For a second Viveca looked surprised, as if she'd never considered the possibility that her mother might be wrong.

Then she brought her drawing straight up to her nose. "Well, maybe," she said. And while Viveca inhaled her pineapple-coconut smoothie costume, Paige looked up at the clock over the door. Lunch was almost over. She had to get to Gavi's table. She reached down into her backpack and gave her lucky rubber lightbulb a squeeze. Then, taking out her secret project, she headed over to Gavi.

Gavi was sitting with Lily and Mack, who didn't seem to know how to handle Gavi being mad at Paige. Lily and Mack glanced up at Paige. "Hi," they both said quickly, and then acted as if their Teddy Grahams and Fruit Roll-Ups were the most fascinating things on earth.

"Uh, I have something for you," Paige said to Gavi. Gavi shared a look with Lily and Mack, and then Paige handed Gavi a small book. The cover was made from colorfully patterned origami paper. "I made it."

"Oh?" said Gavi, and opened the book. The pages were filled with dots and dashes.

"It's a message for you in Morse code," said Paige. "I found the code on the Internet. See? You can match up the dashes and dots with the letters of the alphabet here and decode it!"

Gavi nodded. "Hmm," she said, her lips pursed in concentration. "The first letter seems to be an *I*."

"That's right," said Paige.

Gavi fiddled with the corner of her glasses as Lily leaned in to read the coded message. "And the second letter seems to be . . . an *M*."

"Yep. That's it," said Paige, tapping her foot. Out of the corner of her eye she saw her teacher, looking ready to call the end of lunch. *C'mon, Gavi,* thought Paige. *Decode faster!* She needed Gavi to get the message before they all went back to their classrooms.

"And the third letter seems to be…" Gavi bit her lip, checked the dashes, checked the dots, then double-checked the letters beneath them.

Paige shook her hands wildly, as if she was trying to shake out something icky. She couldn't wait a second longer. "It says, 'I'm really sorry about the Milkshake mess. Your friend, Paige!'" Gavi looked up at Paige. "Sorry about blurting it all out," said Paige. "But I just can't stand another minute of our not being friends."

Gavi smiled. "Yeah…me, too. Mack just told me how you broke up the Milkshake Club."

Paige looked surprised. "I did? I mean, she did? I mean, wait. I broke up Viveca's club?"

"Yep," said Mack. "Well, I think Cynthia Sobkin and some other girls are still in it, but everyone else dropped out. You sure have guts, Oklahoma!"

Paige looked down and shuffled her clogs. "Huh. Well, it wouldn't be fun without Gavi."

Gavi gave Paige a small smile and looked her up and down. "So where is Milkshake?"

"Oh, I'm keeping him at home from now on."

"So you're homeschooling him?" said Lily.

"Yeah, kind of," replied Paige. "I don't think I really

need a sidekick so much. It's more fun hanging out with a good spy. Especially one who's double-jointed." Gavi nodded and cracked her knuckles. "And another thing, you guys," said Paige. "I've decided Oklahoma can be my middle name."

Gavi's eyes grew wide behind her smeary glasses. "Really?" she said. "So now you've got a *super*-secret identity?"

"Yeah, I guess," said Paige. "From now on, just call me Paige."

"OK," said Gavi. "I mean okay, Paige!"

And this time Gavi's smile was so big, Paige let out a huge *"Yee-haw!"* and turned a cartwheel right there in the cafeteria. It was kind of crooked and her hand smooshed straight into some cold Tater Tots on the floor. But still. It was definitely a cartwheel.

Now, if she could just cartwheel her way out of being Viveca's monkey.

Chapter Fourteen
Oklahoma in the Middle

It was D.E.A.R. time, the time of the week when everyone in room 3 had to *Drop Everything And Read*. Paige loved D.E.A.R. time because they could read any book they wanted to. But today it was hard to drop everything and just read. Her eyes kept tilting up from her book to the large pad propped on the easel at the front of the room. On the pad, Ms. Hardy-Wilson had written a list of students' names and the acts they would perform in the Fall Variety Show. Paige's eyes wandered down the plank of names and acts, and by the time she reached the last name, she knew that if she didn't take the plunge now, she might never do it. *Seize the day,* she thought, and, clutching her lucky rubber lightbulb, went over to her teacher's desk.

Ms. Hardy-Wilson was busy searching for something in her Drawer of Wonders, the place where she kept all the things she had taken away from students. Eventually, she gave them back. But today the drawer was a treasure trove of glue sticks, glitter pens, yo-yos, sticky frogs, toy cars, digital games, lip balm, Hacky Sacks, and hair clips. As Paige stared down into the drawer, her fingers tingled with desire to stir the treasure soup just as her teacher was doing.

"Well, hey there, Oklahoma," said Ms. Hardy-Wilson. "And how're you doing this afternoon?"

For some reason, whenever her teacher called her Oklahoma, it felt good. "I was wondering," said Paige. "Um..." She squeezed her lucky lightbulb. "Are we allowed to change our minds about the variety show?"

"Well, certainly," said her teacher. "I think we have you down as an usher. But we can change that. Would you rather hand out the programs? Or sell raffle tickets?"

"Actually," said Paige, "I'd like to play the piano."

Her teacher flashed her big, toothy smile. "Well, ain't that a dinger! Let's go make that change right now!"

"Thanks," said Paige. "But there's one other thing."

"Yes?"

"From now on, could you please call me Paige?"

Ms. Hardy-Wilson looked straight into Paige's eyes. Paige didn't need to look away. Somehow, her teacher's gaze made Paige feel like a true Oklahoma. "Are you sure?" Ms. Hardy-Wilson asked.

Paige nodded. "I'm keeping Oklahoma in the middle."

"Well, I'm glad to hear that," her teacher said softly. "I think it's always good to have a little Oklahoma in your middle." Paige agreed, grinning, as her teacher fished out a fat red marker.

Standing next to Paige at the easel, Ms. Hardy-Wilson squeaked her red marker across the word USHER and squished in the word PIANO. When she lifted the marker off the pad, it looked as if she had created yet another name for Paige: PIANO PAIGE TURNER. Satisfied, Paige squeezed her rubber lightbulb and returned to her desk.

"Oh, so are you gonna turn pages for the piano player?" asked Viveca when Paige returned to her seat. "Get it? Page turner?"

"Yeah, I get it," said Paige flatly. "But no, I'm not turning pages. I'm the player!" Now that it was up there in fat red marker, there was no turning back.

Viveca looked perplexed. "I thought you were going to dance with me . . . and Milkshake!"

Paige gave her lightbulb another good squeeze. "I don't think so," she said. "Milkshake has really bad stage fright. I wouldn't want him to barf all over you."

Viveca's mouth dropped open. Paige picked up her book and found where she'd left off.

"Do you really think you can perform alone without totally freezing up?" said Viveca. "You *need* to be with me." But Paige was busy looking across the room at Gavi peeking over her own book. Gavi flashed her the okay sign, and Paige nodded back. Once more, she glanced at her own name next to the word PIANO. It sure was a dinger. She just hoped it wasn't the kind of dinger that would turn into a disaster.

For the next two weeks, Paige couldn't pass the living room without swooping to the piano and practicing her piece for the variety show. The song was called "Little French Dance," and Paige played it so often her parents had started speaking to the tune of the music:

(Mrs. Turner)   *I'm going now!*
                              I'm going now!
                              I'm going now,
                              Oh, yes!
(Mr. Turner)   *Here are your keys.*
                              Don't worry, dear,
                    I'll clean this kitchen mess.

Paige hadn't realized she'd been practicing that much. But she had to make her fingers super-smart so they would skip along the keys without tripping or stumbling.

"Hey, Paige Turner," Viveca said one day while she and Paige and Gavi were doing flips on the jungle gym. "Who's turning the pages for you at the variety show?"

Paige stopped flipping, and a worried look filled her face. She hadn't thought of that.

"Get it? Paige Turner needs a page turner!" squealed Viveca. She put her hand to the side of her mouth and called out, "Hey, anybody want a job? Anyone want to be the page turner?" But before Viveca could say another word, her hand slipped off the bar and she fell straight down to the mat from the middle of the jungle gym. Paige and Gavi sat on the bars, stunned. Viveca tried to get up, but she'd hurt her ankle badly and couldn't stand on it.

Everyone rushed to the jungle gym and made a big fuss over Viveca. No one had ever seen her cry before, and they stared in silence as Ms. Hardy-Wilson helped her limp to the nurse's office.

"I wonder if she's going to be able to dance in the show," said Paige.

"I doubt it," replied Gavi, flipping down to the mat. "But I'll turn the pages for you."

Paige followed Gavi carefully down to the mat. "Really? *Yee-haw!*"

So every day after school for a week, Paige practiced her music with Gavi. Paige also taught Gavi Cordelia's poem, and when there was time, they spied on Conrad.

"Whoa, it's really smelly!" Gavi said one day when they were peeking into Conrad's room. She was disappointed he wasn't there to spy on, but the smell intrigued her, so she opened the door a little more and took a deep sniff. "I think there's a dead body in there!"

Paige could see that Gavi was already unraveling the Mystery of the Stinky Smell. "Sorry to disappoint you," Paige said, pulling the door closed. "But that's just Conrad's socks."

Chapter Fifteen
Oklahoma, You're On!

By the week of the variety show, Paige felt as if she could play "Little French Dance" in her sleep. One night, she actually did. The whole Turner family came shambling down in the middle of the night to find Paige swaying as she played.

"Come along, Paige," Mr. Turner said, and gently lifted her hands off the keys and guided her back to bed.

When the big night finally arrived, the Turners ate an early supper. Paige's stomach felt like a pinball machine at full tilt, and she could only manage a few bites. *Just as well,* she thought. *Less to throw up.* Excusing herself from the table, she washed her face and then also ran the washcloth over her lucky rubber lightbulb. It had to come through for her tonight—big-time. She brushed her hair and checked her outfit in the mirror, went downstairs and then ran back upstairs to check her hair and outfit once more. When she was all ready, her mother gave her a squirt of cologne and a new purple bandanna to tie around her neck.

"Have you got your music?" she asked Paige just before they left the house.

"Now, don't forget your music!" said her father.

"Yeah, don't do something dumb like forget your music," said Conrad.

Sheesh! It was as if her family was even more nervous than she was.

The evening air in the school parking lot was cool and mellow. As Paige galloped ahead of her family toward the school doors, she breathed in the candied smell of maple leaves. The classroom windows glowed like Halloween pumpkins, and Paige decided on the spot that school would be much more fun if they could always go at night.

At the doors to the cafetoria two students handed out programs. "What a great cover!" exclaimed Mrs. Turner.

Paige agreed and was glad Ms. Hardy-Wilson had taken her suggestion to ask Viveca to do it. Viveca had been more excited about drawing the program cover than about dancing, which she couldn't do anyway because of her twisted ankle. Paige pointed out the names of all the kids she knew who were performing. But the moment she found her own name, what little supper was sitting in her stomach turned to rocks.

"Just remember to visualize your goal!" said her father.

"Yeah, and if that doesn't work," said Conrad, "imagine the entire audience in their underwear eating watermelon." He spit a few imaginary seeds by his side. "Guaranteed—you won't mess up!"

"I'll try," Paige said weakly, and took her place in the first row, where her name, Paige Turner, was taped to the back of the seat. She sat between Lily and a girl with a lovebird that ate spaghetti. Gavi was sitting right behind her. From her chair, Paige could see a sliver of Sanjay behind the curtain. He was working the lights with one of the teachers. While the principal greeted everyone and made announcements, Paige twisted her music in her hands. Swinging her legs nervously, she wished she could hide behind the curtains like Sanjay. The longer she sat, the worse she felt. Her hands grew clammy and shaky. What if her fingers didn't stop shaking? "Little French Dance" would sound like a message tapped out in Morse code: *dit-dit-dah-dit-dah-dah*. She set her program down and squeezed her lucky lightbulb.

First up was Lily. Her act was hamster bowling. She introduced Meep the hamster and placed him inside a clear plastic hamster ball. Across the stage stood three toy bowling pins.

When Lily placed the ball on the floor, Meep's scurrying feet rolled the ball toward the pins. About halfway there, the ball suddenly zigged all the way to the right. Then it zagged all the way to the left and swiftly rolled toward the edge of the stage. The audience gasped. "Watch out, Meep!" yelled a voice in the dark, and just as it looked as if the hamster was going to fly off the stage and crash down, Lily grabbed the ball. But before she placed it back in the middle of the stage, she whispered something into the ball. This time, Meep rolled forward in a perfect straight line and knocked down all the pins.

"He got a strike!" Lily shouted, and the audience applauded wildly. Lifting the hamster out of the ball and cupping him in her hand, Lily took a deep bow.

The next act was Noah Fiedler and his saltine crackers. Noah walked up to the microphone with a plate of saltines, a bottle of water, and a broom. He set the bottle and the broom on the stage and filled his mouth with crackers. Then, with his cheeks bulging, he whistled the song "You're a Grand Old Flag" into the microphone. Cracker crumbs sputtered from Noah's mouth, and the audience clapped along as if it was the Fourth of July. For his finale, Noah took a swig of water and swept up the crumbs. This brought on tremendous hooting and a lot of foot pounding.

But Paige's heart was pounding even harder. And when an elbow suddenly jammed into her, she feared her heart would pop out the other side.

"Pssssst!" It was the girl with the spaghetti-eating lovebird. "It's your turn!" Paige leaned forward. She looked down the row to Ms. Hardy-Wilson, who nodded: *Yes, you're on.*

As she headed for the piano with Gavi, Paige's chest felt too tight to even try for a deep, cleansing breath. She uncurled her music, but no sooner had she set it up on the piano than it slipped to the floor and scattered in three different directions. Noah Fiedler jumped up from his seat and helped them gather it. "Thanks!" Paige whispered to Noah. But as she was putting the pages in order, her lucky rubber lightbulb rolled off the piano bench. Horrified, Paige slid off the bench, squatted down, and peered into the darkness of the cafeteria. "Did you see where it went?" she whispered to Gavi, who was also squinting down at the floor.

"No!" Gavi whispered back. "It just bounced away!" The audience began to shuffle and mumble.

"Paige!" Ms. Hardy-Wilson whispered in a very non-whispery voice. "You're on!"

Paige and Gavi returned to the piano. But before Paige could start playing, she leaned over and checked the floor once more. Where had it gone?

Without her lucky lightbulb, how could she possibly get through "Little French Dance" without messing up?

A sickening wave rolled through Paige's stomach. Then she remembered Conrad's idea and stared out at the audience. Maybe if she could imagine everyone in their underwear eating watermelon, she could stop shaking. The cafeteria was completely dark, and with the spotlight shining on Paige, she couldn't see past row two. It was just light enough to see her third-grade teacher, Mrs. Funkhauser. The teacher whose shoes she'd barfed on.

Paige swallowed the sour taste in her mouth. She took a deep breath through her nose and let it out. She bent her arms like chicken wings. She reminded her shaking fingers to be smart. Then she looked up at Gavi, who cracked her knuckles and whispered, "Move yer keester!" Paige nodded and placed her foot on the pedal. As the opening chords of "Little French Dance" filled the air, Paige's stomach squeezed the same way it had last winter when Conrad pushed her snow tube off the edge of a steep, snowy hill: There was no stopping now.

How Paige ever reached the end of "Little French Dance" seemed a great mystery. It all happened so quickly. She was sure she must've skipped an entire section. She definitely remembered stumbling over one part. But somehow, her fingers had found their way back to the right keys. It was as if they knew the way blind-folded. And now people were clapping and whistling. She didn't remember how or when she and Gavi had left the piano. It was as though she'd dreamed she was taking a bow and had floated back to her seat. But it wasn't a dream. She'd actually done it...without totally messing up or barfing!

When she was back in her seat, Paige's heart bounced around like a brand-new Super Ball. She wished she had magic powers that could make the girl with the spaghetti-eating lovebird disappear. Because more than anything else, Paige wished she was back at the piano, playing "Little French Dance."

This time she would actually hear herself. This time she would remember the zingy happiness of finishing the piece and standing by the piano, taking her bow.

If only!

Mrs. Klonsky was right. The joyful sound of applause made Paige wish she could play "Little French Dance" again and again.

After everyone had performed, the principal thanked the students for sharing their talents and all the friends and families for attending the show. A wave of parents then surged to the front of the cafeteria.

"Congratulations!" Paige's parents shouted when they finally reached her.

"You played wonderfully!" said Mrs. Turner, pulling Paige into a perfumed hug.

Conrad patted her on the shoulder. "Way to go, Nebraska. You sounded pretty good up there. And you didn't freeze up."

"That's only 'cause I didn't have to watch you eating watermelon in your underwear!" Paige said, and spit a few imaginary seeds at him.

Her father said, "See what can you do when you visualize your goal?"

"Right now," said Mrs. Turner, "I'm visualizing some refreshments. There's a big sheet cake and some nice cold punch in the lobby. How 'bout it?"

But Paige was too busy watching a bouquet of flowers moving toward them. She knew there was someone behind the flowers, but the thick crowd of people made it hard to see.

Finally, a familiar face emerged from behind the bouquet. Paige shouted, "Mrs. Klonsky!" The sight of her music teacher made Paige's heart squeeze with happiness. It also brought a wave of shyness crashing over her, and she didn't know what to say.

Mrs. Klonsky, having been tossed about in the warm sea of kids and parents, looked just as uncomfortable. "For you," she said, thrusting the flowers toward Paige.

Paige beamed. No one had ever given her a bouquet before. She breathed in the scent of the flowers and said, "Wow, they're beautiful. Thanks!"

"You played well," said Mrs. Klonsky. "And you remembered your chicken wings."

"I tried to remember everything!" Paige said, flapping her elbows.

Mrs. Klonsky said, "I am proud to be your teacher." Then, turning to Paige's parents, she politely excused herself and disappeared into the crowd.

"Hey, Paige," Gavi called, squeezing her way through the crowd with Mack. "Look what I found!" She handed Paige her lucky rubber lightbulb.

"Good work," Paige said, blowing the dust off. "But I think maybe it's best for squishing."

"That's exactly what I told the marketing people!" said Mr. Turner. "It's good for squishing. And sometimes that's enough! But do they listen to me?"

Just then, Ms. Hardy-Wilson approached the group. She looked a little sweaty and bedraggled but wore a big smile. "I'm so proud of you, Paige Oklahoma Turner!" she said, welcoming Paige into her big bear hug.

"Hey, listen to this!" Mack said, turning to Paige and Gavi. "My mom says you guys and Lily can come with us next weekend to see my aunt Darcy in a show."

"Your aunt's an actress?"

"No. She's a dentist. But she's always done a lot of community theater."

Paige turned to her parents. "Can I go with them? Pretty please?"

"Fine with me, I suppose," said Mrs. Turner.

Mr. Turner asked, "What show is it?"

"It's a musical," said Mack. "It's called *Chicago.*"

"Oh, no!" groaned Conrad, smacking his hand against his forehead.

Paige squeezed her lucky lightbulb and spoke into it as if it was a microphone. "Shi-*CAH*-go," she crooned dreamily. "Now, there's a name with glamour and glitz!" She looked around at the worried faces of her parents and Conrad. And for a moment a little zing of pleasure ran through her as she imagined them all wondering, *Who is this girl going to be tomorrow?*

Paige didn't have the answer but decided she rather liked that. To think there could be so many possible selves, so many Paiges in one single person, just as her teacher had said. It felt great, and she couldn't wait to compose a piece of music about this night. But for now she just shouted "*Yee-haw!*" and led the way to cake and punch, her clogs clomping extra loudly and her whole self full of joy.